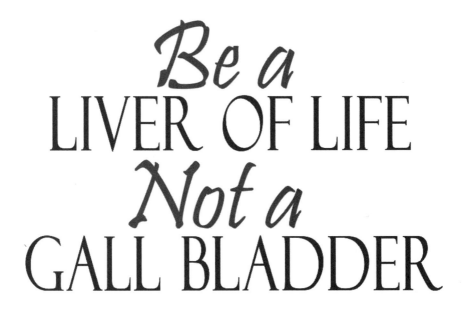

Be a
LIVER OF LIFE
Not a
GALL BLADDER

AN *encouraging, insightful and humorous*
PERSPECTIVE ON PERSONAL AND PROFESSIONAL GROWTH

MICHAEL BROOME

Advantage™

Published in the United States of America
Advantage Media Group
P.O. Box 272
Charleston, SC 29402
amglive.com

ISBN 1-59932-023-1

Printed in the United States of America

Dedication

Sugarpoot and the monkeys.

You are my raison d'etre.

Contents

Please Read Your
INTRODUCTION

Ben Franklin said, "Most people die by the age of twenty-five -- but they aren't buried until they are sixty-five." The fact that you have picked up a book with such a bizarre title as this one has suggests that you don't fit the mold -- you are searching for a more fulfilling slice from life's pie. Thousands of lives have been changed by the information within this book, including my own. I'm confident that you, too, will be a beneficiary.

I haven't written about becoming a CEO, a gold medallist, a number-one sales person, getting rock hard abs, or making a fortune in real estate without putting any money down. Though the principles in this book could assist in achieving these objectives, my purpose is far more expansive. It's about being a liver of life -- improving our character, our attitude, our relationships, our discipline, and our sense of humor. There's nothing we do that can't be improved in some way. It's about being a better boss, a better employee, a better mate, a better parent, and a better friend. By reading this book, you'll learn how to have less stress and more joy, how to establish priorities and live by those standards.

The night Teddy Roosevelt died, an open book was found by his bed. Until the very end of his life, he was an apostle of self-improvement. Regardless of our age or stature, we should continue to hone our life skills. To help you to do so, I've chronicled a multitude of examples, opinions, statistics, facts, jokes, bad puns, and anecdotes. Abraham Lincoln said, "They say I tell a great many stories. I reckon I do; but I've learned from long experience, that people take them as they run, and are more easily influenced through the medium of a broad and humorous illustration than any other way." In keeping with Lincoln's reasoning, I've written in a conversational tone, ignoring some rules of grammar. Often a preposition is a wonderful thing to end a sentence **with.**

I've only written about subjects that I practice. For that reason, there's nothing in here about organization. It's certainly important, but it would be hypocrisy to give advice in this area since my desk looks like a garbage dumpster with drawers. Certainly you won't agree with everything. That's fine, because if two people always agree, one of them must be dead. Unfortunately, some people look for opportunities to disagree and to take offense, especially by remarks intended to be humorous. Before such critics have read very far, I'll have something for them.

Livers of life laugh often and frequently at themselves. They wear a lot of hats: leader, team player, and servant. They set goals for the future, but they enjoy the now. They love people, have noble ideals, and learn from their mistakes. They cherish their relationships and their faith more than their possessions and prestige. This may sound trite to some, but it's not viewed with a jaundiced eye by livers of life -- you'll be introduced to a number of them, mostly through historical examples. There is more wisdom to be mined from past generations whose wisdom has stood the test of time. All of our contemporary values have been influenced by the past in some manner. **To know history is to better understand ourselves.**

You won't read anything so brilliant that it will be chiseled in granite. Some critics of "self help" books claim to have "heard all of these principles." Perhaps that's true since there are few thoughts that weren't previously thunk. However, if critics want to make a valid statement they should say, "I've heard this before and apply the principles 100% of the time." Obviously no one can make such a claim, and that's why we should continue to study the basics. Vince Lombardi started each new season by holding a ball in his hand and saying to his championship players, "Gentlemen, this is a football." Afterwards they practiced things they had done since childhood. Lombardi understood that **by the basics, we succeed or fail.**

Think of this book as advice from someone who has learned a lot from trial, error, research, and from seeking the advice of wiser persons. Books change people more than any other means of communication. They engage you in a wide range of emotions, challenge some of your assumptions, entertain and educate you; all while on your posterior. When reading I hope you dog ear pages and underline so much it causes a librarian to seek counseling.

Thanks

I'm complimented that you are willing to read this book, and hope you adopt many of the thoughts as your own. Upon completion, you'll know me better than some people I've known for decades. At the conclusion you may feel like I feel toward the "Never Lost" computer that guides me on long trips when driving a rental car. The mechanized female voice suggests where to turn, stop, go, and reroutes me when I've made a mistake. When I arrive at my destination, I feel I should send it (her) flowers. The voice actually reminds me of my wife who does all the driving in our family -- my job is simply to hold the steering wheel. As the reader, you hold the wheel and I hope you keep turning to the next page.

Finally, if you are not a person of faith, I ask your tolerance for the occasional references to my beliefs. I make my living speaking to secular business, association and government audiences, and I'm well trained in the appropriate boundaries. However, I do believe a book inherently has more leeway since it's a form of private communication between author and reader.

It's said a clinched fist is like a closed mind -- neither can accept a gift. As the reader, you wouldn't want me to lie or deny the basis for my thinking. To write about the multitude of human issues covered in this book and not incorporate divine insights I've been taught would be a disservice to you, the reader, and to God, in Whom I believe. Frankly, my motive is summed up in the words I want inscribed on my tombstone, **"He was so amazed by God's grace that he could not keep it to himself."**

With exception of those who use religion as an excuse for hate and destruction, I respect everyone's right to believe as they choose. I often quote others who do not share my beliefs. For instance, the French philosopher (and skeptic) Voltaire wisely said, "I quote others to better express myself." Indeed, all knowledge should be considered, regardless of its source. Thanks for your consideration.

1
A Good Thing

You've heard that too much of a good thing can be bad for you but Mae West, sultry star of the silver screen said, "Too much of a good thing… can be wonderful!" Gratitude is a wonderfully good thing that softens the blows from irritations, disappointments, and tragedies. It's not the result of our circumstances; gratitude flows from what we value. People with gratitude exist in horrible conditions and some whining ingrates seem immune to real hardships.

If you want to increase your satisfaction with life, let me tell you about the most fulfilled people I've met and studied. They don't compare themselves to others because they focus on their own plusses. It's been said that the answer to whether a glass is half empty or half full depends on whether you're pouring or drinking. Appreciative livers of life drink daily from the fountain of gratitude. Their credo is the familiar Elvis line, "Ah thank you, thank you very much."

Since we are drawn to envious comparisons from birth, gratitude must be learned. Our first word might be "mama," but our first complete sentence is, "That's mine," or "That's not fair!" Observe nurseries and you'll note the majority of toddler conflicts involve the possession of some toy or food. If you serve ice cream and the scoops aren't equal, you'll be chastised by the munchkin scoop monitors. Are adults different? Any CEO can cite cases of bitter employees who failed to get a raise equal to someone else's. Judging by the recent rash of corporate mismanagement, apparently some CEOs covet bigger "scoops" than they deserve.

Extreme coveters think to want something is to deserve it; to lack it is unjust. Such was the thinking of a former accountant (call him Joe) who kept my books and embezzled money. When asked why he did it, Joe unknowingly used Sir Edmund Hillary's response when asked why he climbed Mt. Everest, "Because it was there." Proof of Joe's covetous nature was a list I discovered where he compared the cost of his possessions with mine, item by item. The Bible teaches that the love of money is the root of evil, but Joe's problem came from his love of my money. Now my wife of twenty-three years, Karen, keeps our books. She says I'll know when money is missing -- because she'll be wearing it.

After reading the first draft of this chapter a friend said, "You don't want to start off writing about coveting because everyone covets, and you'll turn people off." She may have a point, but no one is a perfect example of the principles discussed in this book, including me. However, those seeking to improve their character acknowledge weaknesses and hold fast to their strengths. The challenge is to keep covetous thoughts to a minimum, and when they occur -- expel them.

Maturity enables us to admit when we haven't worked hard enough to deserve some of the things we want. If we were diligent but failed to achieve our goals, maturity helps us accept that life's blessings are not equitably distributed. **Satisfaction should never be determined by comparison.** Regardless of how much coveters acquire, their inner cow craves the grass on their neighbor's side of the fence. Perhaps that's why the poet Robert Frost wrote, "Good fences make good neighbors."

Misfortune Creates Options

Gratitude is more than an appreciation of good fortune. Referring to the sufferings of the South after the Civil War, Robert E. Lee said, **"Misfortune that is nobly borne, is good fortune."** For instance, some years ago Karen and I were devastated when doctors told us we were unable to conceive children. We felt our infertility was a curse. Now, after adopting three happy children, we see our infertility as good fortune; otherwise, we wouldn't have known our kids. What we once considered a curse, we now consider a blessing. A country song says, "Sometimes I thank God for unanswered prayers." If we had the power to go back in time and give birth to the biological children we once prayed for, we would not do so. We'd like to adopt again. Karen wants a toddler but I want a child old enough to mow the grass!

Do I know others who possess something that I lack or have things I feel they don't deserve? Yes I do, and I'd probably be jealous if I dwelled on it. As stated earlier, it's impossible to never have a coveting thought. An old proverb teaches, "We cannot keep the birds from flying over top of our heads, but we can keep them from building a nest in our hair." Likewise, we can keep covetous thoughts from residing in our minds.

To Envy, Observe, or Admire -- That is the Question

There is a difference between observing others and being envious. Each year automobiles improve because of the ideas companies glean from one another. Athletic teams and the military make comparative analyses of opponents' strengths and weaknesses. People with such diverse occupations as farming and teaching make strategic decisions based upon what other farms are growing or what other classrooms are achieving. McDonald's developed a 200-page book for its franchisees detailing everything you need to know about choosing the best location for a restaurant. By contrast, Wendy's sends its franchisees an e-mail with a single sentence --"Locate near McDonald's!"

Observing others' accomplishments is healthy if done from a perspective of admiration or in search of knowledge. Author Ayn Rand wrote, "Admiration is one of the greatest and rarest pleasures." As children we admired home run kings or prima ballerinas while fantasizing that we, too, could be great. Looking for lessons and inspiration from others is essential for achievement. But envious observations are more likely to create frustration than motivation. If envy had a color it would not be green, but rather a dark, foreboding hue.

Problems arise when we have a competitive mentality in our relationships. Either we are critical of those with more, or we try to keep up with the Joneses. Unfortunately, by the time we catch up to the Joneses -- they refinance! Reading magazines such as Better Homes and Gardens can give you great ideas; just accept that most articles are about people with better homes and gardens than yours. **While the envious person resents others' achievements, the liver of life is inspired by their example.**

Frontier Friendship

Coveters cheat themselves out of enjoyable relationships by not appreciating other's talents or assets. Their relationships have more to do with being on the same rung of the social or economic ladder than with being kindred spirits. Author H.G. Wells said the path to social advancement is strewn with broken friendships. It may be more accurate to say it is strewn with broken "acquaintances." **True friends want you to surpass yourself; they enjoy your successes.** I found a wonderful example of this principle of friendship while reading about the exploration of the American West.

Trailblazers Kit Carson and John Fremont discovered passageways that made the settling of the West possible for thousands of families. The hardships they experienced surpassed those of Lewis and Clark. Carson was meagerly rewarded for his contributions. He struggled financially throughout his life on the small pay of an army scout while Fremont experienced uncommon success. Fremont married the daughter of the famous US Missouri Senator, Thomas Hart Benton. Because of the opportunities his father-in-law arranged for him, John Fremont became the most celebrated "pathfinder" of his day. He went on to become a Governor, a US Senator and the Republican Presidential candidate in 1856.

All the ingredients were present for Carson to be jealous of Fremont's good fortune. After years of separation, he was told that Fremont, in addition to all of his other successes, had struck gold in California. Carson's response is particularly impressive considering his poverty and Fremont's "Midas touch." Carson said, "I have heard that he (Fremont) is enormously rich. I wish to God that he might be worth ten times as much. All that he has or may ever receive, he deserves. I can never forget his treatment of me while in his employ and how cheerfully he suffered with his men when undergoing the severest of hardships. His perseverance and willingness to participate in all that was undertaken, no matter whether the duty was rough or easy, is the main cause of his success."

As they said in the Old West, Kit Carson was the type of friend you'd want to, "ride the river with."

Do You Want a Cheap Thrill?

The cheapest thrill available to everyone is to get excited about the good fortune and achievements of peers and family. The Optimist International Creed contains this statement: " to be just as enthusiastic about the success of others as you are about your own." Enjoying others' successes allows you to live vicariously through their lives without the headaches. Like being a grandparent, you get the benefit of loving grandkids without the carpool.

Though selfishness should never be a motive for supporting friends, encouraging others often results in being a beneficiary of your friend's bounty. Two such examples are portrayed in several old movies. In the classic western, *How The West Was Won*, an old woman named Maggie was traveling with a wagon train. Even though she hoped to find a husband on the trip, she allowed the beautiful and younger Miss Prescott to ride on her wagon. Opting not to be jealous, Maggie said, "You're gonna attract men like fish to bait, maybe I can catch one when he swims by," and she did. In *The Sound of Music*, the wealthy Captain Von Trapp's friend, Max, quipped to the Captain while eating his caviar, "I love to be around rich people because of the way I get to live when I'm around them."

Snobs and Snubbers

Livers of life are comfortable around those who are more endowed. As a result, people with various talents are drawn to them. Those who relish others' successes enjoy an enlightening freedom. The circle of people in whom they take pleasure is so much broader than the insecure person whose comfort zone stops where envy begins. Just as some achievers become snobs, it's also true that many "have-nots" snub people they envy. I met a woman who received the, Teacher of the Year award. At first she was ecstatic, but her joy turned to regret when she became the recipient of peer jealousy. She discovered that some people aren't jealous of their peer's success -- as long as they are not too successful.

Emerson wrote, "Everyone is my superior in some way, in that way I can learn from him." Similarly the wealthy nineteenth-century philanthropist Andrew Carnegie had carved on his gravestone: "Here lies a man who was wise enough to surround himself with men wiser than he." Though many acknowledge that someone may be more educated than they are, most people are hesitant to give others credit for being wiser.

To Compare Creates Despair

Someone told me he disliked reading biographies of historical figures because it made him feel insignificant. If he can't handle reading about prominent people who are dead, how inadequate he must feel in the presence of achievers with a pulse! When comparing themselves to others, coveters fail to grasp that they are comparing apples to oranges. It's possible they lack the skills, discipline, or knowledge of the person they envy.

Earnest Hemingway wrote about a rather "manly" form of envy in one of his safari stories. While hunting in Africa, the hunters would gather each evening and brag about their kills of the day. The satisfaction a hunter derived from bagging his trophy instantly diminished if someone brought to camp an animal with bigger horns, tusks or mane. Native American braves must have felt a similar disappointment when they scalped a foe only to discover he was a member of the Hair Club for Men.

Hemingway's hunters assessed the value of their trophies through comparison. Some parents assess their children in a similar fashion and become frustrated if their children don't measure up. Perhaps their children haven't attained what others have achieved athletically or academically. Maybe their kids' gifts lie in the areas of creativity or compassion. Wouldn't you rather have an academically average child with a joyful nature, than a genius who wondered how he came from such a dumb parent?

To look enviously at another's mate is to assume that man or woman would be the same if they were married to us. It's likely that what we see doesn't tell the whole story, like the nearsighted raccoon that seduced a skunk. Afterwards he said, "Beware of what you covet, you might get it."

Ridding ourselves of the albatross of envy frees us to admire something without the need to possess it or to make comparisons. At the core of coveting is the feeling that some thing or some trophy will bring fulfillment. But doesn't the excitement and satisfaction from the acquisition of most things soon diminish -- especially "trophies" acquired in the hope of increasing our importance?

The Princess and The Pauper

Until their deaths, the two most admired women in the world were Mother Teresa and Princess Diana. Princess Diana was on the cover of *People Magazine* forty-four times. Mother Teresa's aged face never graced the cover and she didn't hire a PR firm to remedy the inequity. Her self-esteem was not dependent upon press clippings. She said that in the gaunt starving faces of the untouchables she served, she saw the face of God. **The more we value people, the less we covet things.**

A woman was pushing her baby in a stroller when a stranger gushed, "Oh, what a beautiful baby!" Pushing the stroller aside and reaching into her purse the mother boasted, "If you really want to see beauty, look at her pictures." There's no substitute for some things, nor can they be improved upon. We cheat ourselves when we don't know the difference.

Gratitude Stories

I will never forget the last conversation I had with my mother as she lay dying from cancer at the age of fifty-eight. She said, "Well at least I made it to fifty-eight." At the time I thought, "How could she say that? Dying at fifty-eight is tragic." My attitude was based on a comparison of the average life expectancy of seventy-six years. Later I came to realize that she was not thinking of all she would be missing in life, but of the good things she had experienced and the new life awaiting her. I was angry about the premature ending of her life and she was grateful for the life that encompassed her years.

A phosphorous grenade burned Vietnam veteran and Speaker, David Roever over the majority of his body and grotesquely disfigured his face. He feared his new bride would be unable to love a man whose appearance was so repulsive. Repeatedly he visualized her seeing him for the first time, screaming in horror. When she finally arrived at his bedside, he covered his face and told her to leave. Bending over she kissed him and said, "Don't worry Darling, you weren't that good looking any way."

Laughing, David realized all he had lost was his looks. He hadn't lost his life or his wife's love. As you get older and you lose your looks, hopefully you'll still have your health. If you lose a loved one, you have the memory of your relationship. If you lose your job, look on the bright side -- somebody else found it! I'm not seriously suggesting that we deny life's pain, but a healthy gratitude keeps us from wallowing in misery.

Kurt Warner (winner of the MVP award in the 1998 Super Bowl) and his wife Brenda's infant son Zachary suffered an accident. It left him severely brain damaged as well as visually and physically impaired. Each year on the anniversary of the accident, the family has a party for Zachary. Some may think it is odd to celebrate such a tragedy, but the Warners say this day was a blessing. It was on that day Zachary became so special. Indeed, not only is he special but Zachary is also fortunate to have parents who can find value in misfortune.

From the Mouths of Babes

Another inspiring example of gratitude came from the pen of an eight-year-old girl named Fanny Crosby. Fanny was one of the most prolific songwriters of the nineteenth century and lived to be 95. When she was five years old, a doctor gave her an overdose of medication causing her to completely lose her eyesight. At eight years old she wrote this poem.

Oh what a happy child am I,
Although I cannot see
Resolved am I that in this world
contented I will be,
How many blessings I enjoy
that other people don't
To cry to whine because I'm blind,
I cannot and I won't.

Can you imagine such a mature sense of gratitude from a child? Each of us has the capacity for such an attitude if we know where to look for inspiration. Real joy results not from the absence of sorrow, but from an appreciation of God's blessings. To nurture this attitude in our kids, our family frequently plays the "grateful game." We take turns naming things for which we are grateful and the list can run the gamut from American Girl dolls to indoor plumbing.

It wasn't that long ago that people were as familiar with outhouses as we are with microwaves. Familiarity with such latrines is gone with the wind. On our farm, we have a campsite complete with an outhouse. For our city slicker guests we installed a feature no other outhouse in America has -- a seat belt. A few of the more gullible have actually strapped themselves in.

In a relatively short span of time, our lives have drastically improved. For example, did you know that for every month that has passed since 1900, life expectancy has increased a week? Today more than 70,000 Americans are over 100 years old. We live in such a blessed age, yet some still pine for the "good old days."

When were the good old days? Maybe it was when the first colonists settled at Jamestown or Plymouth Rock. Actually these were the bad old days. Roughly 80% of those who landed died within two years from starvation and disease. More than a 150 years later, in 1776, the average life expectancy was only thirty-six. The smallpox epidemic that began in 1780 took the lives of 120,000 Americans.

A hundred years later, a Nebraska woman captured in her diary the hardships of pioneer life. In one excerpt she wrote that while chopping firewood, a tree fell and pinned her leg against the ground. Bees flew out of a hole in the tree to sting her. She covered the hole with her palm to keep them from exiting. The bees were unable to sting her because her palm was so callused -- and most of us think we work hard.

Some say this is a horrible time to raise children. Yes, problems such as drugs, gang violence, and teen pregnancies have escalated alarmingly. But go to any hundred-year-old cemeteries and you'll frequently see gravestones for children. Diseases such as whooping cough, diphtheria, typhoid, scarlet fever, tuberculosis, polio, and cholera roared through communities taking huge numbers of children in one fatal swipe.

In 1917 World War I began -- in the '30s the Depression -- the '40s World War II -- the '50s the Korean War, and the beginning of the nuclear arms race. The '60s brought Vietnam, campus and urban riots, assassinations, and the drug culture. The '70s produced gas shortages, inflation, unemployment, 20% interest rates and, worst of all in the '70s --polyester leisure suits!

These are The Good Old Days

We've always had problems and we always will, but most of the challenges we face today, even the threat of terrorists, pale in comparison to the horrors we overcame in the past. Today, we eat better than King Henry VIII, travel in more comfort than the Queen of Sheba, and have more recreational options than King Tut. With cable television our access to literature, art, and music would have turned Shakespeare and Mozart into couch potatoes. Advances in medicine and pain reduction have been truly miraculous. George Washington spent his adult life suffering from toothaches. Today, we rarely have tooth pain and yet you never hear anybody say, "My teeth feel great!" Nobody mentions their teeth unless they're complaining.

History helps us appreciate the present by chronicling the difficulties of humanity's past. To lack knowledge of history is like being a capstone with a wonderful view and not realizing you're sitting atop a pyramid composed of countless supporting stones. In his book, *History Of The English Speaking Peoples*, Winston could influence the person who wrote your obituary, wouldn't you prefer that he describe your generosity and service, rather than chronicle your possessions? The truth is -- our choices do write our obituaries.

Big Hair Economics

Interestingly, when I began tithing, my income did not increase as some big-haired televangelists promise, but something more significant happened. **I am more appreciative of what I have, and more wisely spend and invest the remainder.** Wherever you place money in the great scheme of things, it deserves respect -- not disdain, or worship. The most important question is not how much we own, but how much of what we own, "owns" us. If you retain nothing else from this chapter, remember this, -- **there's nothing wrong with being content with what we have, but we should never be content with what we are.**

Each of us has the capacity to experience an increasing level of joy as we mature. You may no longer sleep like a baby, but I'll bet your dreams are more entertaining. Likewise, a maturing sense of gratitude enables you to be more entertained by the everyday little things. A beautiful sunset, a child's laugh, a good book, a snuggling pet, a heartfelt hug, a savored memory -- the list is endless. Lincoln said the Lord must prefer common people because He made so many of them. For the same reason, He must also prefer simple pleasures. So can we.

racial, religious, and political hatred. **Laughter is one of the windows to our soul.**

Feed the White Dog

Churchill suffered from occasional bouts of depression. He referred to it as "that black dog that follows me around." In each of us there are two dogs: a white dog and a black dog. The white dog represents laughter, love, courage, compassion, joy, and all the positive thoughts and emotions. The black dog represents greed, fear, anger, pessimism, hatred, and all the negative thoughts and emotions. We feed the black dog with our negative thoughts and with our positive thoughts we feed the white dog. From the moment we awaken, these two dogs begin to fight. They fight all day long and into the wee hours of the night. Each day the winner of the fight is decided by which dog we feed and which dog we starve.

In the movie, *The African Queen*, a drunken Humphrey Bogart tried to justify his inebriated state as, "only human nature." Katherine Hepburn played a nineteenth-century spinster who was a British Sunday schoolteacher. I love her response to his excuse, "Nature is what we were put in this world to rise above." The following event which happened to me, illustrates her point:

I checked into a Holiday Inn late one night. The clerk told me it was their first night of operation and I was the only person to check in except for three beautiful flight attendants who checked in before me. I went to my room and turned on the light but it didn't work. In the darkness, I walked across the room to turn on a lamp beside the window. Just as I was about to flip the switch, I looked out the window and saw the flight attendants skinny-dipping, in the Jacuzzi. Apparently they thought they were hidden from view because only from my second floor vantage point could they be seen.

Gawking at the women in the dark like a Peeping Tom would have been against everything my mother raised me to do. It would have been against everything my church teaches and everything I profess. In essence it would have been the height of hypocrisy. Of course -- hypocrisy has its advantages. As I stood in the dark spying on these women, something that Billy Graham said concerning lust came to my mind. He said it is not the first look that is the sin, but the second look -- so I thought my first look should last a long time. Truthfully, after wrestling with my "human nature" for a few moments, I closed the curtains and turned on the light.

Are you any different? Haven't you looked at things you shouldn't and tried to justify it to yourself? We're like the little boy who was caught looking at a *Playboy* magazine. His excuse to his father was, "How will I know what I'm not supposed to look at -- if I don't look at it!"

My point is that it's not the first lustful, pessimistic, or jealous thought that is the sin. Sin occurs when we allow our minds to dwell in such places. In ancient Greece the word "sin" was an archery term meaning "to miss the target." **Our thoughts are arrows that can miss the target, and, as a result of our natures, we all sin.**

You, Too, Can Be a Great Thinker

Great thinkers throughout history have disagreed on a variety of topics; however, there is one generally agreed upon premise. American psychologist William James stated it succinctly: "We become what we think about." Roman philosopher general Marcus Areallius said, "Our life is what our thoughts make it," and Lincoln noted, "Most people are about as happy as they make up their minds to be."

Think about it. When you are depressed, your mind is dominated by debilitating thoughts. When you are joyful, your mind focuses on positive thoughts. It doesn't take a brain surgeon to understand that while dwelling on negative thoughts, a happy mood is unattainable, and vice versa. The influence of your thoughts is inescapable. To harness that power for your mental health, exercise dominion over your thoughts and starve your black dog.

As stated earlier, when we experience real tragedy and disappointment, we need to feel the pain and anguish. During his sophomore year at Harvard, Teddy Roosevelt lost his father whom he adored. At the age of twenty-five, both his mother and his wife

There's A Bad Mood A-Rising

To varying degrees we are influenced by the people with whom we associate, the books we read, and the things we watch. It's difficult to maintain an affirmative attitude when we are inundated with an overload of negative. The world throws so much depressing news at us that we must consciously counteract that news to achieve a balanced view. I surveyed the evening news and found seven out of ten news items to be negative, two were neutral, and only one was positive. That is seven negatives to one positive. If journalists were objective, wouldn't they have more balance? Unfortunately, the media (and many people) share an unhealthy inclination to focus on the bad.

Whenever possible, we should reject influences that bring us down and associate with those who renew our spirits. As children most of us were highly influenced by our peers, and as adults we aren't much different. Dangerous to our psyche are people who belittle their spouse, backbite their bosses, gossip about their neighbors, and whine about life. I know a guy who can brighten up a room just by walking out of it. Like the cynical Peanuts character Lucy he dispenses lots of scathing comments and unsolicited opinions and seldom has anything good to say. I've watched people back away from him like he had industrial-strength halitosis. If you wouldn't let such people steal money from your purse, don't let them rob you of joy by force-feeding your black dog.

Of course there are some individuals we have to deal with such as surly customers, cranky relatives, or maybe even a hormone-erupting moody teenager. Mark Twain's advice for dealing with such youth was when they turn thirteen, put them in a cracker barrel and feed them through the hole in the side. When they turn sixteen, seal up the hole!

Real life is not so simple. When we are unable to reject the negatives in our lives, we should follow the advice of the children's gospel song which proclaims, "This little light of mine, I'm gonna let it shine." Our light can brighten the dark side of others' natures.

The actor Joel McRae captured this "little light" principle with his description of Will Rogers. "He had an influence over everything he touched. The key word is 'glory.' He glorified everything. When he came to the studio -- the behavior on the set improved, the attitude toward America, the attitude toward foreigners, the attitude toward colored people, the attitude toward Jews, he could do all that without ever preaching, just by his example. -- And, in an overall sense, just by his example he glorified God. This man affected nearly everything I have ever done, including making me behave sometimes when I otherwise might not have, just because I would want him to think well of me."

It's rare to find such an uplifting person, but nothing should keep us from striving to exude such attributes. Let your character shine like a beacon of light for others.

We'll never be perfect, but when trying to improve the light of my character, I'd rather ride a rocket to the brightest star and only reach the moon, than bounce on a pogo stick and crash my head on the neon sign over the Black Dog Saloon.

Put in a more poignant way, the poet Robert Browning wrote, **"Ah, but a man's reach should exceed his grasp, Or what's a heaven for?"**

Extremely Extra-Excessive Exaggerated Exuberant Optimism:

Can positive thinking be overdone? Indeed it can. A motivational speaker told a woman that her husband was sick because he thought he was sick. He said her husband should leave the hospital, go home, and repeat 1000 times a day, "I think I'm well, I think I'm well, I think I'm well." A month later the motivational speaker saw the woman and asked, "Has your husband been repeating, "I think I'm well"? She said, "Yes, but we buried him because now he thinks he's dead."

The best examples of excessive optimism are those in denial: salespeople who don't like accountability, parents who don't want to admit a child's drug problem, couples who pretend their marriage is fine when a volcano is preparing to erupt, people who keep spending money when they're barely able to make the minimum payment on a large credit card debt etc.

Hitler was a master at denying reality. As Germany was bombed by Allied forces, Hitler stated the enemy was doing him a favor by destroying buildings he planned to demolish after Germany won the war. He claimed it would make his post-war town planning easier to achieve. Another example was his response to the disastrous invasion of Russia. German troops were unable to move forward because melting snow and spring rains made the roads impassible. Unwilling to admit his blunder, Hitler rationalized to his generals that the weather delay was good; otherwise his army would have gotten too far ahead of their supply lines. The reality was that Russia then had time to regroup and to prepare an offensive that expedited Hitler's defeat.

Hitler's rationalizations were not affirmative thinking, but rather were desperate denials. Reality-based optimism admits problems, tries to correct injustices, apologizes for wrongs, and acknowledges sorrow. A guy I know is an incredibly enthusiastic and positive person -- at least outwardly. When a mutual friend was stricken with terminal cancer, he avoided visiting the friend by explaining, "I just wouldn't know what to say." His shallow optimism was a mile wide, but when confronting one of life's harsh realities, it was only an inch deep.

Lisa Aspenwall, a University of Maryland psychologist, won $50,000 from the Templeton Foundation for her research demonstrating that optimists are more willing than pessimists to read bad news about their health habits and to learn about their failures on tests. "Pessimists may not want to know bad news about themselves, because unlike optimist, they don't think there is anything they can do about it," she says.

Get Real

George Bernard Shaw said, "No one can be happy all the time. If they were, they would probably be miserable." Acknowledging that life is difficult is not pessimistic. I don't know about you, but everything in my world is not always "great". I get mad, feel lonely, and emotionally down. This doesn't happen frequently but I'm not immune. At such times my wife asks, "Who licked the red off your sucker?"

Mature joy is not instantaneous. Instant joy is almost an oxymoron. It can fade as quickly as it appears. It has no roots, no way to nurture itself through droughts. Sometimes depression can be healthy. To suppress bad feelings when they are justified can cause other problems to surface later. You'll never be able to escape the feelings that result from life's trauma, nor should you want to. Only a callous, unconcerned jerk could sail through life with no remorse or sadness from hardships or from witnessing the pain of others. **Though we feel pain, faith enables us to live through it, and eventually to rise above it.**

I Was An Onion

In my twenties, I was an onion. When you peel off one layer of an onion, you find another layer. Peel off that layer and you have another and another and another until you get to the center of the onion and you have nothing. Once you peeled away my layers of positive thinking, career, hobbies, friends, possessions, and you got to my core, there was nothing. I had no relationship with God. These layers had some worldly value, but they did not provide answers to the eternal questions -- what was the ultimate purpose of my life and where would I go when I died? I wasn't an atheist. I acknowledged God's existence and bowed my head when people said prayers; after all, I was a Southerner! I saw God as some abstract entity floating out there in the twilight zone. When I stumped my toe I called out His name, but not in the manner that creates a relationship.

Now the oft-used cliché, "Let Jesus into your heart," is no longer a cliché to me. He's not a crutch; He's a whole hospital. I don't claim to have all the answers, but I'm no longer clueless. Yes, positive thinking is better than negative thinking, but without God it's like eating bread made without yeast -- all you get is a dry chunk of Melba toast. It's edible -- but how much more satisfying is a soft steaming loaf of freshly baked bread? **Prayer elevates our mind from the tyranny of trivial thoughts.** It enhances our belief that we have value, that we are loved, and that God will see us through the most difficult circumstances.

Our prayers should be far more than mere rituals occurring only at meals or on special occasions. We should have an ongoing dialog with God throughout the day -- seeking His guidance, thanking Him, feeling His love, and when deserved, sensing His displeasure. Though I have felt His presence, experienced His guidance and trembled at His grace, I've never heard God's audible voice. Sometimes when I yearn to feel His presence, He seems to be absent. But that's understandable since many people in the Bible experienced the same yearning. After all, God is not a telephone operator waiting to promptly answer our every call. I don't know if (or how) you communicate with God, but if He speaks aloud and answers your every question -- you may need medication.

Know Your Raison D'etre

Comic W.C. Fields said, "Everybody's got to believe in something…so I believe I'll have another drink!" Indeed, those who lack core beliefs will strive to find something to fill the void. St. Augustine said 1800 years ago that God made us for Himself, and our hearts will be restless until we find Him. If our life starts and ends with us, it's a very small circle with nowhere else to go. The most balanced people I've met are people of faith. They know who they are and why they are here. **When you grasp the answers to these questions, loving life comes naturally.**

The French have a saying, "Raison d`etre" meaning, a reason to be. Those who believe they are part of a master plan find it easy to feel gratitude toward the designer. If we are only the result of a random chemical coincidence, there is little reason to have gratitude toward a silent, uncaring universe. Atheism gives no eternal hope if our final purpose is only to become worm dung. The most insightful bathroom graffiti I've seen lampooned existentialist philosopher, Friedrick Nietzsche:

"God is dead." -- Friedrick Nietzsche
"Fred is dead." -- God

With a world of evidence pointing toward intelligent design, it takes more faith to believe in atheism than to believe in God who designed it. The odds of DNA occurring by chance would be similar to a tornado hitting a crayon factory and leaving all the crayons in separate piles, each according to their color. Refusing to acknowledge God's hand in nature is like looking at the presidential figures on Mt. Rushmore and saying, "It's amazing what erosion can do!" Only an illogical faith birthed by denial could say we are solely the result of hydrogen and carbon molecules accidentally makin' whoopee.

You have a purpose. There is more to our lives than what we see.

Fight The Good Fight

A poet wrote, "Two men look out of prison bars; one sees mud, the other sees stars." Livers of life may find themselves in prison, ill, bankrupt, or persecuted but their attitude enables them to rise above their circumstances. When Gandhi was imprisoned he remained content. He sang, spoke kindly to his captors, and busied himself by weaving clothing for the poor. By contrast, Hitler was imprisoned near the beginning of his political career. He wrote his autobiography *Mien Kamph*, in which he spewed venom and planned his tyranny. Gandhi's attitude resulted in India's independence and Hitler's hatred brought Germany's destruction.

The Apostle Paul was imprisoned and beheaded by Roman decree. Caesar was probably unaware of the execution of such an insignificant person. He had far more meaningful concerns with the affairs of his empire. The most powerful person of his age, Caesar's name alone struck fear in the hearts of his enemies. He was worshiped as a god, his every need attended to, his wealth beyond measure.

Compared to Caesar, Paul was a nobody: a poor, persecuted member of a fledgling religion. A vagabond who traveled from town to town depending on the kindness of strangers, his only vocational skill was that of tent maker. He died with neither fortune nor fame. The only things he left behind were the relationships he formed and letters he had written.

"This place is loaded with snakes and they're covered with great big ticks!"

Literally four times more people die every year from bee stings than from snakebites. Logically, people should be more afraid of bees, but nobody ever asks, "Do you have any killer bees?" The old cowboy philosopher was right when he said, "People ain't logical. If they were logical, it would be men who rode sidesaddle"

Yum, Yum Eat em Up

If you have a recurring worry, write down all of the possible solutions. Listing the solutions helps imbed them into your consciousness. An ancient saying teaches, "The weakest ink lasts longer than the best memory." Keep the list in your purse or wallet and when the fear rears its ugly head, concentrate on the solutions instead of being so hung up on the problem.

A training film was made about coping with fear. It documented the story of a woman whose greatest fears were of heights and water. She conquered her phobias by parachuting into the ocean.

When I was small, the biggest fear in my life was a neighborhood bully named Gary. One day he punched me, so I ran home crying to my father who said, "Son, don't be afraid of anything unless it can eat you. And if it can eat you, then try to eat it." The next day Gary pushed me down and sat on my face, so I sank my teeth into his buttocks. He ran home screaming with blood on his shorts. His parents told the neighbors that I was a cannibal. But I discovered a profound truth -- bullies don't pick on cannibals.

What about you? Do you face your fears and worries, or, do you let them nag at you like a festering wound? **When we fail to take action, we increase the odds of our fears occurring.** Jewish tradition teaches that Job said, "That which I feared has come upon me." Oppressive worries rob us of confidence, logic, and focus, which impair our ability to act decisively.

Example: a salesperson is so afraid of rejection that the customer picks up on her lack of assertiveness and her nervousness. The customer isn't comfortable talking to someone so unsure of herself, so the customer says, "I'm just looking." The salesperson says to herself, "I knew I wasn't going to make a sale." She has fallen victim to her self-imposed limitations.

Teddy Roosevelt said he became a courageous man by repeatedly telling himself he was courageous even when he was not. Our response to situations is generally the result of the mental habits we form. Every new thought in the brain creates a neurological pathway. Repetitive thoughts follow the path of least resistance, which is the neurological trail left by the previous thought. That's why the more we repeat something, the easier it is to memorize. People with addictions are more easily enticed because the previous repetitive experiences left more than a trail; they left a neurological highway on which pleasure-seeking thoughts travel.

Triggers (Synapses) ignite the brain's thoughts. An alcoholic, who frequently drinks while listening to a certain song, finds his desire triggered when he hears the same tune. A spouse repeats a nagging comment we've heard many times and it triggers the same angry response. Though we may blame our spouse, we choose to react in anger, thereby creating a habit. Sow a thought, reap a habit. We condition ourselves through repetition; it's the heart of change. Use repetition to create good habits and to change your bad ones.

A Dog Tale

Remember the classic experiment in which Pavlov conditioned his dog to salivate by ringing a bell each time it was fed? When he rang a bell and withheld food, the dog drooled since it was conditioned to associate food with a ringing bell. Pavlov named the dog Sal (short for salivary). Because Sal was a Dalmatian, he was eventually given to the fire department. Unfortunately, whenever he rode on a bell-ringing fire truck, he arrived at the fire drenched in saliva. People never petted Sal because they mistook the foam around his mouth for rabies. As smart as Pavlov was, he could have solved Sal's problem if he had simply taught the dog to spit.

Unlike a dog, with conscious effort we can influence our responses by self-imposed conditioning. For instance, I used to overreact whenever my wife was late driving home. Her cell phone was of little help because the reception in our area is poor.

I finally accepted that her anti-punctual nature was not going to change, and that my worrying benefited neither of us.

Now when Karen is late, I remind myself the odds are a thousand-to-one that she is in danger and to "fear not." In fact, saying, "fear not" is now a conditioned response when a worry enters my mind. Did you know the Bible contains 365 verses with the phrase "fear not"? That's exactly one "fear not" for every day in the year. On the extra day that comes with a Leap Year it's best not to leave the house.

Good Stress

Stress can enhance our performance. Athletes use nervous energy to propel themselves to a higher level of performance. Boxers are so keyed up before a match that they never step into the ring yawning. Our problem arises when we don't have an outlet that burns our nervous energy. During a hectic workday, a brisk walk during lunch can be invaluable, especially when accompanied by invigorating music. Backing away from responsibilities, if only for a few minutes, can be rejuvenating.

Learn the art of taking, "one-minute vacations." Close your eyes and visualize some fun or exciting thing you've done in the past, or plan to do in the future. Appreciating a good story or laughing with gusto makes for potent one-minute vacations. A hearty laugh can be more rejuvenating than a full body massage. *(Well almost.)* I have a network of friends and we call each other during work to share jokes. As soon as the laugh is over, we frequently hang up and get back to work.

Thomas Edison and Winston Churchill were early advocates of what we call today "power naps." They kept beds near their offices and learned to fall asleep and awaken quickly. Their work schedules put beavers to shame. Long after becoming senior citizens, they continued their high levels of productivity.

You may be thinking, "My boss will be thrilled when he sees me telling jokes and taking power naps." Perhaps your work environment won't accommodate naps, jokes, and lunch aerobics, but exercise is something you need to do if you want to reduce life's anxieties. If you think you don't have time, consider that our present president and our past four presidents were all advocates of daily exercise. Surely, if they could find the time…

You Can Do It

If you don't enjoy exercise, it's only because you haven't found the type suited for you. I hate to jog and before I started regularly exercising whenever I saw joggers, I felt guilty. Guilt prodded me to try a number of exercise machines. Only in America will a guy spend $2000.00 on a treadmill and the same amount on a riding lawnmower!

If you don't work out, there are some stress-burning cardiovascular exercises you can learn to enjoy. Surely you know people who, after years of slovenly lifestyles, became exercise enthusiasts. The magic exercise fairy didn't tap them with her energy wand. **The desire to change their lifestyle became greater than their desire to live the same old way.** They focused on the results more than on their resistance to physical exertion.

Perhaps a rowing, stair-climbing, bun-burning machine is right for you. If it is, you can buy slightly used machines at a substantial discount from my attic. Maybe bicycling, tennis, or swimming will become your passion. My love is power walking on nature trails with leg weights, a 40-pound backpack, 30-year-old ski poles, red hiking socks, and army boots. I prefer walking in nature because in public I look like a dork.

Everyone has a "trigger" that will light their fire to exercise. Perhaps the wake up call comes from your doctor, or from positive peer pressure of friends who workout with you. My motivation began when I looked into the mirror and asked Karen if she thought I needed to loose my spare tire. She said, "That's not a spare tire, that's a triple-belted radial with mud grips."

If you exercise regularly, be glad you discovered the life-enhancing habit that evades so many people. If you are contemplating exercise, you must believe that by sticking with it sweating will become a joy -- something you cannot imagine doing without. You actually begin to crave the stress-reducing endorphins your body produces from exercise. By experimenting, you can find the exercise that will trigger your inner athlete. Teddy

Roosevelt, a staunch advocate of exercise, coined the phrase, "the strenuous life." I have the words displayed in several places and they often stimulate me to act.

You may not be good at sports, but your body was made to move. Exercise is an important component of balanced living. It's cheaper than psychologists' fees and healthier than a double martini. Coupled with the right thoughts and attitudes, exercise will take you to a higher level in the quest to be a liver of life and not a gallbladder.

The Rabbit Factor

Do you sometimes feel like the rabbit in Alice in Wonderland who said, "I'm late! I'm late, for a very important date. No time to say hello, goodbye, I'm late, I'm late!" With all our technological advances, the price we often pay is a constant sense of urgency, a frenzied scramble. When rushed, we should ask ourselves, "Is this justified? Will it matter if the task before me takes a little longer?" If the answer is yes, then do the task with a calm resolve. As the tortoise taught the rabbit, **speed is seldom as important as consistency.** We should never lose our desire to respond quickly to urgent needs, but the only person I've read about who got all of his work done by "Friday" -- was Robinson Caruso.

Having a calm resolve is not to advocate a slack work ethic like I've seen at a local fast-food restaurant. One employee is so slow that if he had a footrace with a pregnant woman, he would come in third. He's clueless in understanding that our competitive economy is largely based on fewer people, doing more, in less time. The results aren't always pretty, but it beats the alternatives like corporate bankruptcy or socialism.

American Can-Do

A friend of mine, proud of his Italian heritage, tells an amusing story about his first visit to Italy. He couldn't wait to see the land of his forefathers and meet, "my people." Upon arriving in Rome, he immediately took a stroll. The first locals he came upon were construction workers who appeared to be on break. They were renovating an ancient cathedral. Unaware that the renovation had been going on for over a decade, he innocently asked when they were going to be finished. Recognizing he was an American by his accent, one of the older workers waved his hands in the air and shouted, "You a @*! STUPID Americano, what's it a-matter when-a we through. We a-finish when we a-finish -- and what-a business is it of-a yours anyway?!!"

Indeed many cultures do lack our American sense of urgency. The adventurous nature of our forefathers who risked all by leaving their homelands and starting anew apparently was passed down genetically creating our culture of "get it done."

During the Revolutionary War Abigail Adams, the wife of future President John Adams, reported that a British General was shocked to see the size of the defensive breastworks the colonists had put up in one night. He exclaimed, "My God, these fellows have done more work in one night than I could make my army do in three months!" If the colonists had had a "Don't worry, be happy attitude," today we'd be drinking tea with our crumpets…. Cheeri-o!

Remember the words from the theme song of the television show *Rawhide*: "Head 'em up, move 'em out, move 'em out head 'em up, keep them doggies rolling..." That same American attitude enabled World War II's George Patton to move more men and equipment farther in less time than any other army in the history of warfare, resulting in a speedier end to the war in Germany. You can bet Patton suffered from stress, but his stress resulted in our victory.

It's true that our fast-paced culture needs to smell more roses, but we didn't become the leader of the free world by squandering time and imitating cultures that think hard work gets in the way of life. Americans have stress because we accomplish more. The only way to completely eradicate stress is to reside six feet underground. Stress accompanies most significant contributions to our world. All historical figures suffered from stress at times because they chose to make a difference. **Life's stresses are unavoidable, but self-induced anxiety can be substantially reduced.**

Notice the word, **reduced**. To think life could, or should, be stress free is foolish. Stress reaches throughout our society, from urban traffic jams to sleepy rural hamlets as the following joke demonstrates:

What makes the noise, bang, bang, clopp, clopp ...bang, bang, clopp clopp? Answer: *An Amish drive-by shooting.*

All Stressed Up

Yes, we have too many neurotic cell phone addicted, beeper carrying, gorge-while-you-drive, horn honking, multitasking, obsessive Americans. She rushes home, listens to her phone messages, checks her e-mails, faxes her broker, loads her laundry, microwaves a Stouffer's and relaxes by drinking her instant slow roasted, genuine-artificially-flavored- original-imitation, domestic international coffee from a Wedgewood Styrofoam cup. (The French would love this!)

I get a little irritated when other cultures critique our American life style. For instance the French disparage our culture's hastiness. In France they're proud of the leisurely way they eat in restaurants, but I think it's because their service is so slow. The only rush many foreigners seem to be in is to immigrate to America. Foreign critics say all we do is rush around trying to make more money. Ironically, the hardest working Americans are usually immigrants who came from these "non-materialistic" cultures. Our socialist critics would be more motivated if they lived in economic systems that didn't overtax its citizens and rewarded initiative, self-reliance, and cowboyism.

This is not to justify our society's neuroses. Rather, we should acknowledge that stress is part of our modern life -- but it can be managed. If your health, relationships, or joy are consistently being harmed by stress, you have the capacity to make the necessary changes. Years ago I realized the necessity of slowing down. One indicator occurred when I was late for a flight and I rushed all over the house like a madman searching for my keys. The neurotic nature of my frenzied search became evident when I yelled to Karen for help and discovered the leather key holder was clenched between my teeth.

When I began a career as a motivational speaker, our PR material said I was America's youngest motivational speaker and I practically lived on the road. Though it took years, I finally realized that less travel meant more life. Now, I'm America's most "unmotivated" motivational speaker. (Actually I enjoy speaking more because I'm not burned out and I do a better job because my interests have broadened.) Knowing your priorities helps you decide how much stress you are willing to undergo, and what you are willing to do (or undo), to achieve balance.

Confucius Says

Our Western culture could learn from Eastern philosophies that teach the importance of doing everything wholeheartedly. When you work, *work*. When you rest, *rest*, and when you play, *play*. Doing things halfheartedly causes stress. Children have the innate capacity to be totally absorbed in their activities. Watch them on a playground hanging from monkey bars, playing on swings, or chasing each other. They are totally absorbed in the moment. When I am fishing with my young kids, they never say, "I just can't get my mind off my homework." How often do you allow yourself to be absorbed in a carefree moment? When was the last time you lay down in the grass and tried to pick out faces in the clouds?

Often it's not the amount of time we spend seeking solace, it's the restful diversion we achieve from whatever time we spend. Many workaholics return from a long vacation stressed out because they never quit thinking of their responsibilities. When Karen first started aerobic walking with me on our farm, she constantly pointed out fences that needed mending, roads that required scraping, trails that needed clearing, etc. In frustration I finally barked, "Just enjoy the walk, and as for the unfinished chores... FORGETABOUTIT!!"

Now she is more likely to point out a bird instead of a birdhouse in need of a paint job. When we learn to exercise, to rest, and to play with focus, we will feel rejuvenated when it's time to work. Living halfheartedly drains our soul and we end up feeling like a car battery that supplied power all night to the interior lights.

The Wise Custodian

Once I arrived at a meeting to deliver a speech and observed an elderly custodian setting up several hundred chairs by himself. He must have been about seventy years old with a head full of white hair. As the people began to arrive, he worked so fast that he looked like a video in fast forward. After setting up the chairs, a stage light went on the blink. He ran to get a ladder so he could climb up to the ceiling light. After changing the light he was told that the meeting was ready to start and there was no microphone. He bolted down a long hall, returned with the mike, and finished setting up the chairs.

When I approached him backstage, he was leaning against the wall with sweat dripping off his brow and trying to catch his breath. I told him that was more work than one person should have to do. His response was memorable. It was not funny, but it was very wise. He smiled and said: **"Every mule thinks his wagon's da heaviest."** Just like an ornery mule, how often do we act as though we are pulling the world's weight on our shoulders?

Harry S. Truman - The S Was Not For Stress

On the eve of the 1948 elections, all the polls and political pundants confidently predicted Harry Truman's defeat. For an incumbent president to lose is a humiliating experience. If it were your election night, wouldn't you stay up for the election returns? Not Harry. As always, he went to bed early and went right to sleep. In the middle of the night, aids woke him and said he had lost New York, which was the most important state for a Democrat to win. He responded, "I'm going back to sleep. Don't call me anymore." At 4:30 AM he was again awakened and told he had won. Truman did not worry about things beyond his control, nor did he fret over a decision once it was made. Perhaps it was these abilities and the fact that he was an avid walker that enabled him to live to be eighty-eight.

On April 8,1965, Ulysses S. Grant was suffering from a debilitating migraine headache. He was fearful of losing the opportunity to surround Lee's army and end the war. Throughout the day Grant was barely able to function and the pain kept him up all night. The following morning a messenger told him that General Lee wanted to discuss terms of surrender. Grant wrote in his autobiography that his headache instantly disappeared. The same brain that caused his migraine created pleasure rendering endorphins that cured his pain.

On one of his expeditions, Daniel Boone and a companion took refuge during a driving rainstorm under a horse blanket. Cold, wet, and hungry, his friend complained, "I believe you would be satisfied to remain here forever." Boone replied, "You would do better not to fret about it, but try to content yourself with what we cannot help." Similarly, Teddy Roosevelt exhausted his guide, Joe Ferris, while hunting buffalo in the Badlands of South Dakota. For a week it rained incessantly and all they had to eat were biscuits and rainwater. At the height of the guide's misery Roosevelt exclaimed, "By Godfrey, but this is fun!" **One person's stress is another's pleasure.**

Our minds can make or break us. Aren't there things that once caused you stress that you now handle with ease? Remember how anxious you were the first time you tried to drive a car, or before your first date, or that first day at a new job? Just as those events are no longer bothersome, you can reduce your present anxieties. Mastering them won't happen overnight -- you've spent years conditioning yourself to respond stressfully to certain situations and it will take time to reverse the habit.

Don't Tread On Me

I'm convinced that the most common cause of stress is not from overwork -- rather it results from our interactions with others. If we allow them to do so, the angry spouse, crying baby, irritating customer, nosey neighbor, or cranky boss are far more likely to impact our peace of mind.

In days of old there was a village simpleton who carved beautiful eagles out of blocks of wood. The city council commissioned him to carve a giant eagle for the town square. When the eagle was completed, the unveiling occurred to the delight of a large crowd. Never missing the opportunity to hog the spotlight, the mayor quieted the crowd and said, "Being a Phi Beta Kappa graduate, it is hard for me to understand how a moron such as yourself can carve a magnificent eagle from an old stump." Ignoring the rude nature of the mayor's statement, the wood carver smiled and simply said, "Well, Mr. Mayor, I just cut away everything that don't look like an eagle!"

Likewise, we can learn to control our angry responses by making light of another's insensitivity. Teddy Roosevelt's wife Edith had a strong since of propriety. She was often irritated by the outrageous things Teddy would say and do, like his skinny-dipping in the Potomac River. "You only have to live with me," she periodically quipped, "while *I* have to live with *you*!"

It's healthier for your blood pressure to disarm your antagonist than to respond in kind. When my daughters or my wife becomes angry with me, I've reduced their hostility by impersonating John Wayne and saying, "Well Darling, you sure are pretty when you're mad." Or if Karen is irritated and orders me to do something, I'll exclaim with a wimpy voice, "Oh, I just love it when a woman takes charge!" Some might view this as condescending, but it generally lightens the moment which is better than fighting fire with fire.

A Civil Response For Civil Rights

Rosa Parks, the mother of the civil rights movement, refused a bus driver's demand to give up her seat for a white person. When he threatened to have her arrested, she could have screamed, "You redneck honky, I'm not going to take it anymore." Rather, when the driver told her he was calling the police, she took the high ground and calmly said, "You may do that." She refused to allow her antagonist to control her reaction.

In 1776, the twenty-one-year-old American patriot Nathan Hale said to his British executioners, "I regret that I have but one life to give for my country." It would have been understandable had he spent his last moments cursing his hangmen, but he took the "higher" ground.

Livers of life understand that we may all be victims of injustice, false accusations, or rude behavior, but they recognize we have the ability to control our response to drenching rains, egotistical mayors, bigoted bus drivers, or vengeful Red Coats. When others make your temper boil, they control your thermostat.

Guilt Is Good

If guilt or regret is causing you anxiety, there is a solution -- but, first you must recognize the difference between guilt and regret. Regret is the memory we have of our mistake. By itself, it is of little value. Many criminals regret committing a crime only because they were caught. What do Adolph Hitler, Osama Bin Laden, and Oklahoma City bomber Timothy McVey have in common? They were guilt-free. These three stooges of self-righteousness are excellent examples of what happens when there is no capacity to feel remorse.

Contrary to some contemporary views, guilt can be an enlightening emotional thought process that motivates us to listen to the angels in our nature rather than the devils. Dr. June Tangey at George Mason University, has studied guilt for thirteen years. Dr. Tangey says, "Those who feel guilty tend to be understanding and forgiving and are able to build strong relationships. Guilt motivates people to apologize or to do something to fix the harm they have done."

Guilt becomes debilitating when we continue to commit the same act, making little or no effort to repent. In such cases the fault lies not with our conscience, but with our lack of discipline. Blaming guilt as the cause of our stress and shame is akin to blaming the messenger when we don't like the message. Guilt is the messenger that makes us do things we may otherwise have postponed doing or not done at all. **Guilt is one of the consequences we pay for wrong actions. Without consequences the world would be in chaos.**

Misplaced Guilt

Guilt can be misplaced. We often feel compelled to apologize for things outside our control such as being ill, the rude behavior of others, or getting stuck in traffic. When you visit other people's homes, haven't you heard many women with incredibly busy lives apologize because their house is not in perfect order? When they were growing up, they were apparently influenced by seeing thousands of commercials showing women whose lives were fulfilled because they could see their reflection in their sparkling dishes and floors. Perhaps the floor cleaner named Mr. Clean should be called Mr. Guilt.

A classic example of obsessive guilt is found in the life of Martin Luther. As a young monk he was so obsessed with guilt that he went to confession for as many as six hours a day. He would ransack his memory searching for every minute sin, reviewing his entire life until the confessor grew weary. One such encounter resulted in the confessor's telling Luther that if he wanted Christ's forgiveness, he should confess something like blasphemy or adultery instead of so many triviums!

Later Luther came to realize that regardless of how much effort he exerted, he could never be sinless; his only hope was to depend upon the forgiveness that God promises through repentance. His grace is extended to us even though our sins may be so grievous, there is nothing we can do to compensate for our foul deed. In fact, **God loves us so much, not only does He forgive our sins; He forgives us knowing that we will commit many of those same sins again.** (Think about the amount of love that requires.)

Amazing Grace

What do we do when the person we've wronged refuses to forgive us, or is dead? Jesus taught that when we sin against others we sin against God. Yes, we should ask forgiveness from the person we have wronged, but remember: even if they do not forgive us, God's forgiveness is promised when we genuinely repent.

No one understood this better than John Newton, who wrote the words to the most well-known gospel song of all time, Amazing Grace. Newton served as captain of a slave ship and was responsible for transporting thousands of slaves. The life he led beginning as a cabin boy and rising up through the slave trade was one of debauchery. Not only were the slaves sexually and physically abused while in transport, but many were killed for the slightest infraction. Eighteenth-century drawings show how slaves were literally packed like sardines into the bowels of ships, having to wallow in their excrement.

As a result of his Christian conversion, Newton left the slave trade and joined the fight against slavery. Because the slaves he transported were spread throughout North America and many were dead, it was impossible to seek forgiveness from all the victims. His only hope was the redemption promised by a forgiving God. This should give you a better understanding of the words to the song when he wrote.

> *Amazing grace, how sweet the sound*
> *that saved a wretch like me.*
> *I once was lost, but now I'm found,*
> *'Twas blind, but now I see.*

If you suffer from guilt, surely your deeds could not match the heinous nature of John Newton's, yet he was able to find redemption. Because of God's grace, amazingly, so can we.

Stress and Insecurity :
Hitler Was a Weenie

Hitler was the prime example of a seemingly confident person who was insecure. He boldly claimed his ascension to power resulted from a divine will and his unequaled brilliance. Despite his appearance of self-assurance, Hitler was easily ruffled by criticism or by suggestions that he was wrong. His screaming fits and his bullying nature masked his feelings of inadequacy. Hitler's tantrums proved the old saying, **"An empty wagon makes the most noise."**

He never danced because he refused to do anything that demonstrated his ineptness. Hitler's exercise regimen was an amusing example of his insecure obsession with his image. To create the false impression that he was physically fit, his driver let him out at the top of streets that sloped downward. Throngs of onlookers watched "The Fuhrer" walk vigorously downhill until the road took an uphill incline, where his driver secretly waited to pick him up. In Texas they have a saying aimed at the urban cowboy: "Big hat, no cattle." Healthy confidence does not manifest itself by deception. **A healthy confidence acknowledges that, although you may not always be the best, you will give it your best.**

Harry Truman stated this principle in an oral biography entitled *Plain Speaking*. He said, "Well, I never thought I was God; that's one thing for sure... I never had the notion that I was anything special at all; even though I got the job at the White House, I didn't. And I never got the notion that there weren't a lot of people who could do whatever it was better than me...**All that ever concerned me was that I wanted to do it as best I could.**"

No one could accuse the feisty Truman of lacking confidence. Yet he understood that if you think you are irreplaceable, stick your fist into a bucket of water and quickly withdraw it. Just as the void quickly fills, so will our place be filled. Understanding this is not evidence of a poor self-esteem, it is a sign of a balanced ego.

People with a healthy confidence improve their performance by admitting weaknesses and doing something about them -- not by thinking they are faultless or the only rooster in the hen house. This may sound like a contradiction, but there is nothing wrong with having a big ego. Ego drives people to accomplish great things, to go the extra mile, to take risks, and to assume responsibility. The real danger is when our ego has us. Egotists overestimate their abilities and importance -- they think the sun rises just to hear them crow. Frankly they need to be told that regardless of their importance, the number of people who attend their funeral will be determined by the weather.

The Adams Family

If our self-esteem is based on being the best, what do we do when we lose our position or retire? Some former U.S. Presidents suffer dejection because they are no longer the head honchos. John Quincy Adams avoided this syndrome by doing what no other ex- president has ever done; he ran for Congress. Adams was quite satisfied serving his country in what some would view as a demoted position in the House of Representatives. He was happy in this capacity because he did not compare his new station in life to his former. His self-esteem was not dependent upon a title -- it was enhanced by service to his country.

John Quincy Adams' father, former President John Adams, was the ringleader of the rebel rousers during the Revolutionary War. If they would give up the revolution, King George offered amnesty to all the members of the Continental Congress, except for John Adams. The King wanted Adams hanged for his rebel-rousing blasphemies against the Crown.

Obviously anyone who so aggressively opposed the Crown was not lacking in confidence. Yet as an old man, Adams understood the importance of acknowledging one's limitations. He wrote, **"The longer I live, the more I read, the more patiently I think, and the more anxiously I inquire, the less I seem to know..... Do justly. Love mercy. Walk humbly. This is enough."**

The Godfather

The opposite of this philosophy was found in the life of Mafia boss John Gotti. He beat three criminal prosecutions in his first five years as a Mafia chieftain. Rather than hide his underworld crimes as his predecessors had done, he flaunted his ill-gotten gains and activities. Gotti held weekly meetings of his "captains" at The Raventie, a Manhattan social club, as tourists gawked. He was frequently overheard discussing his crimes in public. He dressed and acted the part of a flamboyant, macho crime boss who exuded confidence and felt above the law. A car driven by a neighbor accidentally killed his twelve-year-old son. Police said the neighbor was not at fault, but the neighbor mysteriously disappeared.

Gotti's careless discussions of his crimes were tape recorded which eventually lead to his conviction. In prison, Gotti's arrogance resulted in two inmates severely beating him for calling them racial names. He became bitter and complained that his family had abandoned him. Like comedian Rodney Dangerfield he felt, "I don't get no respect." The empire Gotti had built crumbled, and he died in prison of cancer, a shell of the pompous man he had been.

4

You Talkin' Ta Me?

A woman from New York City drove through the South and stopped at a South Carolina Welcome Center to use the restroom. A Southern woman who was seated in the next stall asked, "Hi there Honey, how are you today?" She had heard Southerners were friendly so she replied, "I'm OK, how about you?" Her Southern stall mate replied, "I'm just fine as sunshine. What are you plannin' for this wonderful day in Dixie?" Hesitantly the New Yorker replied, "I'm driving to Miami, where are you going?" The Southerner irritatingly said, "Honey, some rude Yankee keeps interruptin' me. I'll call you back!"

As the New Yorker discovered, conversations lacking a mutual interest end up in the toilet. We've all begun conversations and discovered the other person had no interest in us. Bell Telephone once surveyed 500 telephone conversations to determine what words were most frequently used. The most commonly used word was "I": it was used 3,990 times. When talking too much about ourselves, the only thing we learn is how to lose someone's interest. We are all guilty of this to varying degrees.

Teddy Roosevelt wrote a book entitled, *The Roughriders* which chronicled his experiences during the Spanish American War with the cavalry regiment he formed. He put special emphasis on the Roughriders' famous charge up San Juan Hill, which propelled Roosevelt into the national limelight. A critic said Roosevelt wrote "I, me, and my" so often in his book that it should have been named, *Alone On San Juan Hill.*

Me, My, and I

Play a game with a friend. Start talking to each other but avoid using the personal pronouns, "I, me, or my." You'll be amazed during a five-minute conversation how often you will catch each other using these pronouns. There is nothing wrong with saying "I, me, or my," but the game makes us aware of how much our conversations revolve around ourselves. Focus on the other person, event, or idea and your communications will be enhanced.

When telling about an experience, it's generally best to keep the story brief and avoid petty details. Don't be like the plane that kept circling the runway and eventually crashed because it ran out of gas. Our conversations will also end in disaster if we don't remember that others' attention spans are generally pretty short, especially when we are talking about Number One. Like the guy who on his first (and last) date with a girl said, "That's enough of me talking about me. Let's give you a chance to talk about me."

The Braggart

An applicant for a job with our company wrote on her resume that her previous employer had been a mortician. She boasted about her performance in a manner that sounded like a murder confession from a gruesome Stephen King novel. She claimed, "In only one year, I 'single-handedly' doubled the funeral home's business." She apparently was unaware that some accomplishments are better left unsaid. Similar to Stephens King's grisly claim that his success as a writer of scary stories was simple: "I have the heart of a ten-year-old boy… on my desk in a jar."

A fine line exists between bragging about something you've seen or done, and merely talking about it. Feeling pride in your accomplishments is natural. You're not failing as a communicator every time you talk about yourself. An old Southern saying advises, "It's a poor dog that won't wag his own tail." Truly modest statements are seldom perceived as bragging. Just be aware of **what** you are saying, **why** you are saying it, to **whom** you are talking, and **how** they perceive your comments.

When accomplishing something eventful, it's better for people to find out through the grapevine than to flaunt it. Whom would you respect more -- a guy who constantly brags about his black belt in karate, or a guy who never mentions that he has one? Then one day, to everyone's surprise, he demolishes a mugger who was robbing an elderly woman. Braggarts have few friends and they generally have to associate with other boasters with whom they trade an "I for an I."

Bombarding people with "I, me, and my" is not limited to conversations about accomplishments. We should be particularly careful when talking about possessions. Having quality possessions is fine, but "things" don't create a worthwhile respect from others. A genuine interest in people does. If you make a lot of money, drive a great car, have a vacation home, or win awards, that's wonderful. But, seldom talk about it and if someone asks, speak briefly. To say less is to say more.

People seek relationships with modest persons. **Being a "self-made person" is great as long as you don't worship your maker**. I once read that only successful people admit to being "self-made." The problem with that statement is that no one is self-made. Truly successful people realize that in addition to hard work, their success results from others' influence and from God's grace. So strive to achieve something worth bragging about, *but don't brag*.

An Exception To The Rule

There are exceptions, of course. I enjoy bragging about my expensive clothes. When someone compliments my suit, I love to show them the fine stitching, the quality of the fabric, the label, and boast about the retail cost. When a look of disdain settles over their faces, I add, "by the way, this suit cost ten bucks at Good Will!" It's true. At their deaths, many wealthy people's clothes are given to charity. If my "pre-owned" suits had a logo, it wouldn't be a man on a polo horse ... it would be a man in a casket.

Just remember that people with character are more interested in talking about ideas, books, experiences, and positive things about people -- **so keep conversations about your possessions to a minimum** - unless you shop at Good Will.

Name-Dropping and One-Upsmanship

Seeking status by whom they know, name-droppers are dying to impress others by their acquaintance with someone who is popular, wealthy, or famous; often they exaggerate their closeness. If you are friends with a well-known person, you don't have to hide your acquaintance **but don't inject their name into a conversation to make yourself look like a big deal.**

Akin to this communication's fault is the habit of interrupting others to demonstrate your knowledge. The Latin term for the trait should be, **"ego interruptus."** Regardless of how little they know about the subject being discussed, the guilty interrupt knowledgeable people with some vaguely related minutiae. I heard someone interrupt a Super Bowl winning quarterback who was demonstrating the proper way to throw a football by asking, "Did you know footballs are made of pigskins?" Little did this interrupter realize that it's far more impressive to give someone your total attention than to insert some tidbit. When people who practice ego interruptus tell what they know, they usually demonstrate how little they know.

Another conversational faux pas is called **"one-upsmanship."** No doubt you've had conversations with people who always have a story to top yours. When we were in college, a friend told me I did this when we talked about the outdoors. If he described how cold it was when he went camping, I invariably recalled the time I camped when it was colder. If he told me about catching twenty fish, I reminisced about the day I caught thirty.

The fact is, we've all had a number of unique experiences worth sharing, but it's frequently better to hold back a story, relinquish the stage, **and let the storyteller's adventure be the focus of attention.** Tell your account some other time when it doesn't diminish theirs. (Though I still tell about a twelve-pound bass that broke my line and got away. Since it got away you may wonder how I know its weight? Answer …. The fish had scales.)

Profanity was completely absent in Native American language before the influence of Europeans. Just as profanity was not found in certain cultures, some people exercise the discipline to abstain. Among the many amazing aspects of Robert E. Lee's character was that he never used profanity. Similarly, Ulysses Grant never cursed. Perhaps the memory of his logistical difficulties during the war with Mexico caused Grant to write in his autobiography, "I am not aware of ever using a profane expletive in my life. But I would have the charity to forgive those who might do so, if at the time they were trying to drive a team of Mexican pack mules."

During the Revolutionary War, General George Washington issued an order that any man heard to take God's name in vain would be whipped. He set this standard because he saw it as utter hypocrisy to ask for God's help to achieve victory and not respect the use of His name. If these men who were under the incredible torment of war could exercise restraint, surely it's also within our capacity.

Profane Twain

Since many traditional values have eroded, it's little wonder profanity has become an accepted practice in many circles. Fortunately there are still many circles where it's as out of place as a seersucker suit at a power lunch. If profane people only knew how foolish they appear, they would curb, if not stop the habit. Mark Twain once let loose with a long string of curse words in the presence of his wife, who never swore. In hopes of showing him how disgusting it sounded, she repeated the words back to him. Twain responded, "You've got the words right but not the tune!"

Mark Twain and General George Patton were frequently profane. Though men of great intelligence and accomplishment, their bad language probably resulted from their ill tempers and frequent depression. Ugly words are the result of ugly thoughts and emotions. **"Dirty water does not flow from a clean well."** The more vulgar the expression used, the more out of balance the person is.

I found an amusing article in a law enforcement manual that defined acceptable police conduct when arresting a dangerous criminal. Police were allowed to punch, kick, beat with a club and if absolutely necessary, shoot the assailant -- but it was not permissible to curse the thug!

Though profanity is still not justified, it's understandable that during times of anger, frustration, or pain a majority of people (including me) may curse. But, to compare one who rarely uses profanity to one who is constantly vulgar is like comparing someone who occasionally drives a few miles an hour over the speed limit, to someone who drives 120 miles an hour through a neighborhood. Both are errors but the latter is an intentional disregard for others. Profanity does for the professional image what garlic breath does for a doctor's bedside manner.

I have spent a good deal of time in the midst of people from every level of the socio-economic strata: from working beside minimum wage laborers, to years of consulting with the leadership in various levels of business, education, and government. Though profanity exists everywhere, the higher you go up the ladder of achievement, the less you hear it. Likewise, the lower you go, the more often it's used. The constant profanity in prisons and combative daytime TV talk shows demonstrates that profanity thrives among the ignorant. Most participants on violent talk shows are so dumb, if you gave them the F, they still couldn't spell Fheonix.

To livers of life, the profane are not considered more mature, cool, intelligent, likeable, funny, or hip. Like flatulence, it's something you should ignore but not endorse. The following is a list of the TOP FIVE STATEMENTS you won't hear regarding profanity:

1. **I'd like to give you a raise, but you don't cuss enough at our customers.**
2. **Since you called me a vulgar name, am I to assume you're not happy with me?**
3. **Mr. President, your State of The Union address needed more four-letter words.**
4. **I want to marry someone who can teach my children to cuss like sailors.**

and that I would continue to do so. "But," I said with a smile, "in remembrance of you, I will say 'she' --- whenever I refer to the devil."

This comical response was meant to ease the tension. It solicited laughs from observers but my antagonist failed to see the humor. I'm not always so quick witted but I had previously heard a similar retort and mentally filed it. A guest at a dinner party told Mark Twain how impressed he was that, regardless of the topic debated, Twain had a witty comment. Twain said he merely manipulated the discussions around the topics about which he could be witty. Similarly, a critic said Churchill spent the better part of his life preparing his "extemporaneous" remarks.

We should never be surprised when others disagree or criticize us; it's part of what happens when humans interact. The best politicians are prepared for this; it keeps them from becoming too defensive. Former President William Howard Taft demonstrated how to gain the upper hand by acknowledging your deficiencies.

Taft weighed 335 pounds. Once at a public gathering Chauncey Depew, a noted orator, pointed to Taft's stomach and asked what he was going to name the baby. Taft replied, "If it's a boy, he'll be a junior. If it's a girl, I'll name her Helen. But if, as I suspect, it's only gas, I'll name it Chauncey Depew."

It's A Guy Thing

Though Will Rogers was a humorist, he never told jokes with a punch line. His humor had to do with making fun of present situations and people. Teddy Roosevelt had been the recipient of many Rogers' jests, and when the two met for the first time, Rogers said, "Well, I hope you're not going to put me in jail." Roosevelt laughed heartedly and said, "Don't be afraid you will hurt my feelings. When you can use my name to your advantage, go to the limit!"

There is such a thing in the corporate world as a, "Good ole boys network." For women to gain acceptance, it's helpful to learn the art of the barb -- relating to one another by trading humorous cuts. When most men congregate, it's a major part of their communication and camaraderie.

At class reunions, women tell each other how good they look and guys frequently make fun of each other's weight gain or baldness. At my reunion we gave a prize to the guy who lost the most hair and a number of contestants were awarded "Honorable Mention." An inebriated former classmate got up in my face and said, "I bet you don't even remember me." I said, "I don't remember your name -- but I do remember your breath." He laughed, but I doubt most women would.

Just as men need to be sensitive in their communications with women, many women could enhance their male relationships by indulging in humorous repartee`. The domineering personality of Texas war hero Sam Houston was often brought to bay by his mother in-law, Nancy Lea. During their debates she was fond of telling him, "You may have conquered Santa Anna, but you will never conquer me."

Former British Prime Minister Margaret Thatcher is an excellent example of a strong, independent woman who could give and take humorous barbs. She maintained her classic feminine persona whenever participating in the critical and boisterous style of British Parliamentary debate. She advised, "To wear your heart on your sleeve isn't a very good plan. You should wear it inside, where it functions best."

More Retorts For Your Mental Fort

Lincoln was a master at using humor to lessen the sting of his opponents' criticisms. When running for the Senate against Stephen Douglas, Douglas told the audience that he had known Lincoln since they were young men in Springfield, Illinois. – "when Lincoln worked behind a bar and sold whiskey." Lincoln replied, "But the difference between Judge Douglas and me is just this, while I was behind the bar he was in front of it."

He further stated, "I long ago gave up my post but he tenaciously holds to his."

In Lincoln's first bid for Congress he ran against a noted minister Peter Cartwright. No one had more humble beginnings than Lincoln. A petty campaign lie tried to discredit Lincoln to a group of rural voters by alluding to his aristocratic relatives who were visiting him. Lincoln's response was to say that only one relative had visited him in Springfield and he was arrested for stealing a jew's-harp.

On another occasion while he was riding from town to town as a circuit lawyer, a drunken man who was brandishing a gun threatened Lincoln by saying, "I swore that if I ever saw an uglier man than me, I'd shoot him." Instead of being insulted or arguing with the drunk, Lincoln smiled and remarked, "Mister, if I'm uglier than you, fire away." Sometimes it's better to agree with a fool.

Apologizing -- Just Do It

You can defuse many arguments by simply admitting when you are wrong. When we stand corrected, we stand tall. Learn to swallow your pride and say, "I was wrong," or "I made a mistake." When Douglas MacArthur served as the Army's Chief of Staff, he used his influence to thwart the expansion of the air force. After Pearl Harbor was bombed, MacArthur realized his error and apologized to the renowned fighter pilot Eddie Rickenbacker with whom he earlier had exchanged harsh words over the issue. Considering that MacArthur was not known for humility, he gave an admiringly candid admission, "I probably did the American Air Force more harm than any man living by refusing to believe in the airplane as a weapon of war. I am now doing everything I can to make amends for my mistake."

One reason General Robert E. Lee is held in such high esteem is because of his humility. At the battle of Gettysburg, Lee's army failed to break the back of the Union Army. History has shown that Lee could have blamed the failure on a score of excuses: lack of supplies, poorly fed men, hesitating commanders, etc. Instead, as the bloodied troops struggled back to the Confederate lines, Lee rode out alone to meet them and said, "All this is my fault; I, and I alone, have lost this battle."

(The numerous historical examples may seem redundant, but repetition is the heart of implementing change. The history of human relationships demonstrates that certain lessons need to be repeated again and again. People tend to remember stories more than theories or rambling dissertations. Aesop's fables, the tales of Homer, and the illustrations of Jesus gave insights that are as effective today as they were originally. The various examples

are given in the hope of targeting situations applicable to each reader.)

While he was teaching a course at the Virginia Military Institute, Stonewall Jackson sternly disciplined a student for giving the wrong answer to a question. He believed this was evidence that the student had failed to study. Later, while sitting at home, Jackson realized that the student's answer was correct. Though it was in the middle of the winter and late at night, he walked some distance back to the institute and summoned the student. The nervous student arrived, and to his astonishment, Jackson apologized.

A final example from the annals of Southern chivalry occurred in 1858 in the U.S. Senate. Mississippi Senator Jefferson Davis became embroiled in a heated debate with Senator Judah Benjamin. Davis made insulting remarks to Benjamin, but the following day before the entire Senate Davis apologized. Acknowledging that he had been "dogmatic and dictatorial," Davis said his display of emotion was unacceptable and that he "felt kindness and respect" for Senator Benjamin.

Mea Culpa and Duels

We'll never know whether Davis' apology was heartfelt, or whether he apologized because Senator Benjamin challenged him to a duel! Early in his political career Abe Lincoln was challenged to a duel and told that he could choose the weapon with which to do battle. He said, "I choose cow dung at five paces." He later learned to apologize with more heartfelt sincerity.

In his classic Lincoln biography, Carl Sandberg described an incident during Lincoln's presidency. Colonel Scott from a New Hampshire Regiment came to Lincoln's office one night to ask that he intervene in the Secretary of War's decision to send him into battle. A great battle was forthcoming, and the Secretary said every officer was needed. Scott's wife had just died and he needed to make arrangements for his wife's funeral. She had nursed Scott in a hospital from battle injuries, and on her return home she was drowned when the steam- boat on which she was traveling sank.

It was late Saturday night and after listening to his story, an exhausted Lincoln uncharacteristically said, "Why do you come here to appeal to my humanity? Don't you know that we are in the midst of a war? The suffering and death press upon all of us. Am I to have no rest? Is there no hour or spot when or where I may escape these constant calls....you must not vex me with your family troubles. Why, every family in the land is crushed with sorrow but they must not each come to me for help. I have all the burdens I can carry. Go to the War Department, your business belongs there."

Colonial Scott returned to his hotel room full of despair at the realization that his wife would not receive a proper burial. Early in the morning, he heard a knock at the door. There stood the president, who took Scott's hands and holding them broke out: "My dear Colonel, I was a brute last night. I have no excuse to offer. I was weary to the last extent; but I had no right to treat a man with rudeness who had offered his life for his country, much more a man who came to me in great affliction...I beg for your forgiveness." He arranged for Scott to go to his wife's body, took him to the steamer in his carriage, and wished him God speed. It would be difficult to find a more complete apology. Lincoln acknowledged his mistake, asked forgiveness, and took action to correct his error.

Why is it so hard for people to apologize? Or, if they do apologize, they add a "but" on the end. "I'm sorry but you did this," or "I made a mistake but it's not my fault." Adding "but" on the end of your apologies makes them as effective as adding a "but" to your compliments. I made that mistake at a party when Karen heard me say, "My wife's weight is the same as the day we got married... but it's in different places." When giving compliments or apologizing, we should keep our "buts" to ourselves.

Bury Your Pride

One time a friend of mine died and I was unable to attend the funeral due to a previous commitment to deliver a series of speeches. Some time before we'd had an unresolved conflict. A cloud of depression and guilt hung over me while I was driving to the airport, and I didn't feel like going anywhere to give speeches.

As I was boarding the plane, I said a simple prayer asking God for some encouragement. Ten seconds after the prayer, I walked to my seat and seated right beside me was a priest! The Las Vegas odds of such a coincidence must be extraordinary, but I felt it was the result of divine intervention. Goose bumps literally jumped up on my arms. I said, "I can't tell you how glad I am to see you." He looked me right in the eyes and said, "Sorry, no speak English."

The most he could say was that he was from Lithuania. I was so depressed I had to listen to my own motivational CDs! This true story is not meant to be sacrilegious, but to acknowledge that our prayers are not always answered in the way we want. The rest of the trip was depressing at best, but I came to terms with the mistake I'd made with my friend and realized that some other relationships I had needed mending. If I'd been able to talk with the priest and he had offered absolution, the result would doubtfully have been the same. It appears God knew that time was needed to mull over my transgressions.

Isn't it true that some of your greatest lessons resulted from mistakes you've made, relationships you've blown or lost through death? No relationship is perfect; at times every human bond will be tainted with misunderstanding and anger. When these moments occur, livers of life strive to be as patient with others' faults as they want others to be with theirs.

Don't Wait

A woman's husband died and left her the beneficiary of a million-dollar life insurance policy. Several months after his passing she was relaxing by the ocean at a posh island resort. Contemplating the million dollars she had received, she thought, " I miss him so much...I'd give ten thousand dollars to have him back!"

Unlike that woman, the time is coming when many of the people you really do care about will be gone. The death of loved ones, friends, and associates often seems so unreal, so distant, so removed from our daily concerns. But the day of reality will arrive. Unless we are constantly aware of death's eventuality, we will not treat our relationships as the precious gifts they are.

For that reason, if there are people you love but seldom tell,

For example, over half the companies who were in the Fortune 500 list twenty-five years ago are not there today. But, how can that be? If experience creates competency, then once a company makes it to the top, wouldn't it remain on top because of their experience and expertise? The answer is no. One reason the Fortune 500 list constantly changes is that once many companies reach a certain level of success, they begin taking employees for granted, and employees react by taking customers for granted. Labor and management resist change. They become satisfied with mediocrity, apathetic about customer service, and eventually their customer base erodes like an ice cream cone in a sauna.

Similar apathy occurs in many marriages after a number of years. When they are dating, most guys jump to open doors for their date. After years of marriage they still open doors for their wives… but only when she's moving heavy furniture. Of course, apathy can also happen on the woman's part. On the honeymoon she wore Victoria's Secret, but after years of marriage it's flannel Fruit of The Looms. Or, in the beginning she said, "You take my breath away," which becomes, "You're suffocating me!!"

What is it about the human condition that fosters complacency and erosion in relationships? We foolishly assume that relationships are not going to change. Both business and personal relationships should be treated as the valuable and volatile things they are. Time can enhance our relationships if we look daily for ways to be of more service and compete with our past performance. Remember: **all meaningful relationships, especially those in a competitive business environment, require frequent maintenance, and frequently they require high maintenance.**

If It's To Be, It's Up To We

When he played cornerback for the Dallas Cowboys, Deon Sanders injured his foot making it doubtful that he could continue playing. With that in mind, I was impressed to read that instead of showing up for practice and sitting around sulking, he was teaching the younger cornerbacks his tricks of the trade. These guys were after his job, but he saw them as teammates. With your peers, it should be about collaboration, not competition. Don't be concerned about your peers getting a piece of your pie -- **make the pie bigger for everyone on your team.**

In 1924 famous orator and Biblical scholar, William Jennings Bryan, and humorist Will Rogers were hired as newspaper correspondents. They were employed by the same syndicate and covered the Republican convention side-by-side in the press box. Upon their initial meeting, Bryan made it clear he was a "serious" writer. Rogers suggested that by working as a team, they could achieve a more complete coverage; if Bryan thought of anything funny, he would give it to Rogers; if Rogers thought of anything serious, he would pass it on to Bryan. With some hesitation, Bryan agreed.

Will Rogers' wife Betty wrote in her 1941 biography that after the keynote speech, Bryan turned to Rogers and gave a stern critique of the oratory: "The speaker suffered from a premature climax." Betty mused, "Will thought to himself that he would have to give Bryan a couple of good serious reflections to make up for that!"

With whom should you be teaming to accomplish more? A Norwegian Draft horse can pull eight thousand pounds. When harnessed with another, they can pull over eighteen thousand pounds. And when trained to work together, they pull over twenty thousand pounds.

Fictional heroes like Batman and Robin and The Lone Ranger and Tonto demonstrate the advantages of working in tandem to escape peril. A trend in recent years is for many companies to join forces in advertising and marketing, such as Coke and McDonald's, or Taco Bell and Kentucky Fried Chicken. The Revolutionary War would have been a complete failure if not for the financial aid from European benefactors. The joint diplomatic efforts of Thomas Jefferson, Ben Franklin, and John Adams resulted in this success. Though their personalities and talents were extremely different, they achieved what would have been nearly impossible to do on their own.

Alexander The Great once faced a force three times the size of his own army. Standing silently before his men, he picked up a stick and broke it in half. Next, he put two sticks together and easily snapped them in two. Then he put a bundle of sticks together, and

If there is someone with whom you've had conflicts, consider whether you did something to cause this person to mistreat you. If so, then don't just apologize. Saying, "I'm sorry," is easy, but **asking their forgiveness requires even more humility**. You put the power in their hands. Even if your wrong deed was not as "evil" as theirs, seek their forgiveness. If they respond positively, you've gained. If they reject you, then know you did what few people have the strength of character to do.

Apologies are not always appropriate, but seldom will one party in a conflict be totally at fault. Apologizing to someone who caused the greatest hurt may sound foolish, but those who understand real joy know that bitterness is foolish and vengeance is not ours to seek. "Blessed are the merciful for they shall obtain mercy." **The highest form of forgiveness is not forgiving the repentant, it's forgiving those who haven't acknowledged their mistake.** Christ set this example on the cross when He said of His persecutors, "Forgive them, Father, for they know not what they do."

Grace In The Jungle

An incredibly courageous story of grace began in 1950 with a twenty-eight-year-old missionary named Jim Elliot. Elliot committed to go the wilds of Ecuador and make contact with a dangerous and primitive tribe known as the Aucas. Any outsiders with whom the Aucas came in contact were always attacked.

For six years, Jim prayed for the Aucas and made preparations for meeting them. He and four other missionaries landed their plane by a river and built a shelter some distance from the tribe's settlement. In her book *Shadow Of The Almighty* Jim's wife, Elizabeth, wrote that shortly after arriving, "The thrill of Jim's lifetime was given. He took an Auca by the hand. At last the twain met. Five American men, three naked savages." Two days later Jim and his party were brutally murdered by the Aucas.

However, this was only the beginning of the story. Eventually Jim's wife, Elizabeth, her young daughter, and several other missionaries made their own foray into the jungles and gained acceptance by the Auca tribe. Elizabeth befriended her husband's murders, lived among them, and modeled Christ's love.

In an interview years later, one of Jim's murders said that before the missionaries came, the Auca tribe was on the verge of extinction. Because of constant infighting, revenge murders were so prevalent that the population was decreasing. Forgiveness was a foreign concept, but the example shown by Elizabeth and her fellow missionaries changed the hearts of these people. Elizabeth Elliot's life became proof that **mercy is more than an emotion -- it is a choice.**

Even though you forgive someone, you may still harbor some bitterness. This is only human. Few have the ability to instantly wipe the slate completely clean. When we allow forgiveness to replace bitterness, it usually happens gradually. Bitterness becomes like a ship putting out to sea... the closer the ship draws to the horizon, the smaller it becomes until, finally, it disappears.

A Passion For People

Will Rogers said, "I never met a man I didn't like." Of course, Will never met Osama Bin Laden.

When it comes to people, everyone has their preferences. For instance, one of my heroes is writer and theologian C.S. Lewis. He was one of the twentieth century's great writers whose work changed untold lives. Lewis loved mankind but acknowledged ironically that he did not care for the company of small children. He admitted that his discomfort around children was a weakness in his character, but he just didn't enjoy noisy toddlers.

My aunt Francis loved to take care of old people. The more crotchety and negative they were, the more patience she displayed. She had the ability to make Scrooge smile. Most people lack her patience in serving the elderly, but everyone has the capacity to serve some branch of humanity. Whether it's coaching kids, working with literacy programs, or building homes for the poor, all of us can find something worthwhile that makes a difference. Just writing a check to a charity is not enough. Our greatest joy comes from an eye-to-eye, soul-to-soul outreach. Each life you impact initiates a domino effect.

Define Yourself

Our goals define us. They reveal our values, our character, and our dreams.

Goals are road maps that give us:

- a purpose for living
- improve our self-image
- generate enthusiasm
- help us earn and save money
- focus and discover our talents
- increase our service to others
- accomplish more with fewer resources
- prepare for difficult times
- capitalize on opportunities.

The late radio commentator Earl Nightingale defined success as "the progressive realization of a worthy ideal." In other words, once you define your goal and begin working to achieve it, at that point you are successful. Too often we think that success occurs only upon the triumphant achievement of a goal. The joy in achievement should be gained as we are working and not at the end of the rainbow. Think of success as travel. It's foolish to reserve your enjoyment solely for the arrival -- pleasure should be derived throughout the trip. Since yesterday's successes often lose their luster and the future has yet to arrive, **the present is the only time slot we actually experience, improve, and enjoy.**

Recognizing this, you should commit more to the now. If the path to your goal is not enjoyable, the path, and possibly the goal itself should be re-examined. This is not to say that success results in only doing what you enjoy. There should be risks and headaches -- yet the struggles should not be void of pleasure. The small accumulated victories bring more happiness than if we wait for the final triumph. Since you progress one step at a time, make each step count, take time to enjoy them, and your legs will not grow weary.

Your First Kiss

Remember how you planned your first kiss? Before it occurred, you frequently closed your eyes and saw the object of your desire approaching with a protruding pucker. You plotted how the kiss would occur by practicing on a pillow, a picture, a pet. You rehearsed what you would say before and after the lip-smacking event. You thought about the kiss in such graphic detail that you planned when your lips touched -- which direction your nose would go. Even the location where the kiss would occur was planned -- the bushes at the back of the playground, the back of the school bus, the back of the movie theater, the back yard...**first kisses always occur in the back of some place.**

You'd heard about it from peers, been warned of its dangers by elders, and watched movie stars indulge. You didn't want to merely observe; you wanted to be a participant. Once the goal was thoroughly planned and the opportunity arose, you took the plunge. Afterwards, you were either disappointed or you went back for a second dose. The point is, the kiss happened because you dreamed and schemed. You planned and plotted the who, when, where, and how the kiss would happen. You pursued it as you should any goal instead of merely giving it **"lip"** service.

What about now? Are your goals planned as thoroughly as your first kiss, or do they remain vague dreams that never come to fruition? Does each passing year bring you closer to, or father from, their achievement? You've accomplished a number of goals but have you really examined why others remain elusive. Whether our goals are big or small, present or future, easy or hard, the key to achievement is the same.

Get Specific

In target shooting there's a saying, **"aim small, miss small."** It's not enough to simply aim at a target, nor is it best to aim at the bull's-eye. The secret is to aim at the exact center of the bull's-eye (aim small, miss small). Qualify your goals by breaking them down into yearly, monthly, weekly, daily, and even hourly targets.

Helen Keller said, "I love to accomplish great tasks one tiny step at a time." Those steps should be written down with a method to evaluate progress. It's easy to say you are going to save money, but the proof is creating a specific budget and sticking to it. If your goal is to set aside a specific amount for retirement or to make an A in a class, it's too vague to simply say, "I'm going to save more or study harder." Set a specific target of the income you will set aside or how much time you will study, and track your progress on a chart. Obviously this is simple, but because something is simple doesn't mean it's easy. Sacrifice is seldom easy, but it happens when we realize that **wishing changes nothing -- specific commitment changes everything.**

Comedian Lily Tomlin quipped, "When I was young I wanted to be somebody. I should have been more specific." It's human nature to keep our goals vague. Desires such as, "I want a happier marriage," or "I want to find a job that I really enjoy," are only goals when accompanied with a plan. One reason people have obscure objectives is they feel guilty when they don't follow through with specific steps. No one likes guilt. To avoid guilt, non-achievers keep their goals vague and void of deadlines. This allows them to take refuge in the fantasy that things are fine; but "every form of refuge has its price." When reality finally surfaces, their refuge turns into the harsh reality of failure. To reverse this trend, to increase your output, and to get closer to your targets, "aim small, miss small."

Trains Ain't What They Used To Be

Vague goals result from inadequate research, wrong information, misleading emotions, or childish dreams. As a child, I loved my train set. I sat for hours watching it chug along through tunnels, over bridges, belching smoke, and blowing its whistle. It gave my six-year-old ego a sense of control to change the boxcars or switch the tracks at will. Our family moved when I was seven and the set was lost. The remainder of my childhood I suffered from what Freud might have called "train envy."

Several years ago, as the dutiful husband, I accompanied my wife to a shopping mall. As I was waiting on a bench with a herd of other comatose husbands, I gazed into the window of a toy store and was confronted with my childhood delight. On display was a forgotten desire, a lost vision, a sublimated thrill. I became a man/boy with a mission. Since Karen was shopping elsewhere, money was no object. Like a feeding frenzy, I bought tracks, little people, miniature cows, fake trees, bridges, fences, a water tower, and, of course, a train with all the bells and whistles. It took several weeks to set up this miniature world. With each passing day of construction, the anticipation of reliving my childhood days as an engineer grew exponentially.

When the hallowed moment arrived, I took the controls, revved the engine, hit the accelerator and watched the train go round and round. Within five minutes, I was bored out of my mind! My former childish delight could not be revived. Perhaps others could recapture the fun of this hobby, but for me watching a train go in circles was like watching grass grow. (Though my six-year-old son and I did enjoy seeing how many cows the train could run over without being derailed.)

Fortunately this purchase was not a life-altering mistake in decision-making. However, if I had briefly played with a train before making the purchase, I would have saved time, money, and avoided a boxcar full of wifely chastisements for my frivolous expenditure. Make sure your goals are what you really want, not the result of idle whims.

Use Your Brain

Martin Luther said some days he was so busy that upon rising he had to pray for several hours in order to get every thing done. Both our daily decisions and our major life objectives should result from prayerful thought and rational evaluations. Poorly planned career, marital, and economic decisions result in such problems as job-hopping, divorce, and excessive debt. Thinking.... *really* thinking and planning our life is not easy, especially when there are so many things, events, people, and hormones to distract us.

Marriages often begin this way. "Money? Who needs money? We can live on love when we get married," so declared one young couple. Soon after marriage, they argued over finances and their "love" didn't cover the cost of their divorce.

Even people who have been goal-oriented their entire lives can make poorly planned decisions. They've successfully run companies or led organizations with discipline and vision, yet they failed to develop fulfilling goals for their retirement. They may be financially secure, but they didn't plan for the reality of having so much time on their hands. There are only so many rounds of golf, cruises, and social outings before some retirees ask themselves, "Now what do I do?" Like my toy train, **their dream did not match their reality.**

Without well-defined goals for furthering their education, some students choose their college based on such criteria as "It's a beautiful campus," or "It's where my girlfriend/boyfriend is going," or "They have a great basketball team!" They choose their majors based upon reasons with as much foresight as, "Gosh, I just had to pick something," or "I'm good in math so I majored in accounting."

They continue the same poor assessment to acquire a job, a spouse, a mortgage, and 2.3 children. I'm not trying to be cynical or to critique the lives of hardworking people. Many are happy. Still, the sad fact is that countless people fail to achieve satisfied lives when it's within their ability to do so. Emerson said most people lead lives of "quiet desperation." Today it may be more accurate to say aimless distraction -- excessively surfing the Internet or cable channels while their precious life clock ticks away. Such distractions are the true, "opiate of the masses."

Dissatisfaction is certainly not limited to economic levels. Many doctors and lawyers end up disappointed with their careers. An intriguing book by Judge Carl Horne entitled *Lawyer Life,* quotes a California Bar Association survey that found that seventy percent of attorneys "would choose another career if they had the opportunity and – seventy-five percent would not want their children to become lawyers." When I entered college, I wanted to be a lawyer. Fortunately after taking a pre-law course, I discovered the thing I hated about the study of law was -- the study of law.

Researching the right career should not be a chore but a pleasure. If you're considering changing vocations, or you've been downsized, thoroughly evaluate the day-to-day responsibilities before accepting another position. Does the corporate culture mesh with yours? Will the long-range compensation be enough? Is there opportunity for growth, fun, and meaning? Are your skills what the employer really needs? Your ability to meet the employer's expectations is just as important as the job satisfying your needs. Whether it's the employee's or the employer's dissatisfaction, the end result is the same -- frustration that leads to another job search.

It's Never Too Late

If you've been guilty of having vague personal or professional objectives, remember: the past ended last night! Don't beat yourself up over previous decisions. Churchill suggested, "Among the deficiencies of hindsight is that while we know the consequences of what was done, we do not know the consequences of some other course that was not followed." In other words, you may have made an even worse decision than the one you regret. Either way, the past is past. Your present knowledge is the product of the good and bad decisions you've made. In some ways you should be grateful for your mistakes -- they've taught you what not to do. **As a result, you've never been more capable of making wise, accurate and realistic decisions than you are right now.**

Does that mean you should know exactly what direction to pursue? Obviously it doesn't. You might not know exactly what to do, but you know a lot of things to avoid: time wasters, bad influences, and debilitating habits. Stop doing the things you should not be doing. They either slow your progress or completely block the path to discovering what you should do. Clear away the debris and the path becomes clearer. Perhaps all you know is that you want to change. If so, then commit to do all you can to explore realistic possibilities.

Be a Bookworm

Mark Twain said the person who doesn't read good books has no advantage over the person who can't read them. In order to set realistic and satisfying goals, cultivate the habit of reading. Reading helps you make rational decisions. Some say, "It's not what you know, but who you know that counts." Certainly having contacts is helpful, but here's why the statement falls short: The "who" are generally only able to help people knowledgeable of the "what." The "what" is most likely learned by reading. A study of Fortune 500 CEOs found the number one thing they had in common was -- they were rich! Actually, it was large vocabularies -- which grow from reading. Achievers are readers. America's poet laureate Robert Frost lectured at many Ivey League schools, yet he said the most valuable education was self-taught.

By the time Harry Truman was fourteen, he had read every book in the Independence, Missouri Library. Ben Franklin placed so much value on reading that as a young man, while staying in a boarding house, he made an arrangement with the landlord. Franklin stopped eating meat at the boarding house meals and was charged less. He used the savings to purchase books. As a teen, Lincoln carried a book while plowing behind a mule. At the end of a row, as the mule rested, he would take a few moments to read.

In Doris Kearns Goodwin's biography of Lincoln, *Team of Rivals*, Lincoln told a law student seeking advice in 1855, "Get the books and read and study them. It does not matter whether the reading is done in a small town or large city, by oneself or in the company of others. The books, and your capacity for understanding them are just the same in all places. -- Always bear in mind that your own resolution to succeed, is more important than any other one thing."

Even after his term as U.S. President, Teddy Roosevelt's passion for reading continued. On a safari to collect animals for the National Museum he took sixty pounds of books to the African wilds. After shooting a trophy and waiting for the skinners, he sat on the dead animal and read. Soon the books were stained with sweat, gun oil, and blood. When he returned the books to the Library of Congress, imagine the look on the librarian's face.

If we don't habitually acquire knowledge as the world changes, we'll be as out of place as a Hells Angel at a Tupperware party. In school we take many of the same classes as those with whom we will compete in the job world. After acquiring a job, our employer gives us the same training that was provided to our peers. It's up to us to seek knowledge that separates us from the pack. Unique, self-acquired knowledge gives us power, respect, and job security. To lack such knowledge causes the grim reaper of unemployment to hover over our work place. Of course there are no guarantees, but those who keep abreast of knowledge and are still laid off are more capable of landing on their feet and finding new opportunities. Albert Einstein said that education is what remains after you have forgotten everything you learned in school.

Information acquired from inspiring biographies is especially valuable. Biographies don't have to be about people who share your vocation because their lives offer universal insights. When facing a challenge or a question of ethics, I often ask myself, "What would Lincoln, Roosevelt, Lee, or Churchill do?" I've read so much about Lincoln I actually feel like he is a friend of mine. (As I approach the end of each Lincoln biography, I find myself hoping that this time he won't get shot!)

Develop Mentors

Of all the reading that you do, remember the words of former President Calvin Coolidge: "A wholesome regard for the memory of great men of long ago is the best assurance to a people of a continuation of great men to come who shall be able to instruct, to lead, and to inspire." Whatever your quest, surely there are others who have led the way. Do whatever it takes to seek their advice. Offer to provide some service for them. If they are beyond your reach due to fame, distance, time (or they are just a jerk), find someone who is accessible. And don't waist their time when you talk with them; **be brief, be prepared, and know exactly what questions you want to ask.**

Hebrews 13:7 instructs, "Remember your leaders, those who first spoke God's words to you, and reflecting upon the outcome of their life and work, follow the example of their faith." Lincoln was inspired by Washington. Teddy Roosevelt was inspired by Lincoln. Martin Luther King was inspired by Gandhi, and Bill Clinton was inspired by Hugh Heffner.

Everyone is flawed and having mentors is not suggesting that we should worship anyone. Sometimes I find myself admiring the public person, but not the private person. One of the most insightful questions my company asks on our employment application is, "Name five contemporary famous people that you admire." For good or for bad, our heroes expose us. It could be said -- **by their heroes, ye shall know them.**

Give It Up

Harry Truman wisely remarked, "In reading the lives of great men, I found the first victory they won was over themselves. Self-discipline with all of them came first." Once you have identified a goal, the most important question is, "What am I willing to give up to achieve it?" Early twentieth century evangelist Billy Sunday said that the secret to his trim physique was simple -- he always walked away from the table hungry. **Delayed gratification is the granite upon which achievement is built.**

After the Civil War, a woman asked Robert E. Lee for advice concerning raising her young son. Lee simply said, "Teach him to deny himself." For most gain there needs to be some pain. When confronted with the pleasure/pain choice, procrastinators devise countless reasons as to why it's OK to shuffle papers, watch TV, talk on the phone, sleep late, or eat just one more Twinky. Such people pray like this: "Lord, if you carry me to the top of the mountain, I'll slide down on my own."

We frequently postpone action because the task seems trivial or unpleasant. Every time a toad jumps, upon landing he bumps his rump. He doesn't like getting his rump bumped, but it's the toll he pays for getting from point A to point B. Tolls aren't fun to pay, but they are better than taking the longer slower route. When you find yourself avoiding a task, visualizing the benefits creates the discipline to take the bumps. Focusing on the gain is why humorist Erma Bombeck quipped, "The reason I took up jogging was to hear heavy breathing again."

To lose weight, post a picture of yourself on the refrigerator when you were a more desirable weight. Mark Twain didn't know about carcinogens or fat grams, but common sense enabled him to say that the best way to stay healthy was, "To eat what you don't want, drink what you don't like, and do what you would rather not." If Jesus had healed an obese man, afterwards He may have said, "Go fourth, reduce your carbs -- and here's a set of scales." Many people on diets avoid scales because scales represent reality, and those hesitant to make real commitments avoid reality. **Scales keep our desires in check, and desires that have no boundaries become dictators.** For all of your goals, know what you are willing to sacrifice, develop scales to measure your progress, and --

Be Accountable.

There is no guarantee of success, but if you want to get the odds in your favor, make yourself accountable. How many presidencies have been damaged, ministries harmed, CEOs indicted because they didn't surround themselves with people who held them to a higher standard?

Years ago I decided to stop cursing. My wife suggested that any time she heard me curse, I would have to take off my belt, bend over, and let her swat me on the rump. Several days later, we were standing in a long line at a McDonalds. In frustration, I cursed. In keeping with our agreement, I stepped outside, bent over and Karen hit me so hard that I said, "Damn!" It wasn't overnight, but eventually my profanity was reduced to a rare occurrence.

Tom Laundry, former coach of the Dallas Cowboys, said his job was to get his players to do the things that they didn't want to do so that they could be the players they dreamed of being. Great athletes understand the need for an accountability coach -- Examples include Tiger Woods and his father, Earl; Mohamed Ali and his trainer, Angelo Dundee. Interestingly enough, other duos such as Jim Thorpe and his coach, Pop Warner; Mike Tyson and his trainer, Cus D'Amato, worked phenomenally until their separation. As a result of the separation, the careers and personal lives of Thorpe and Tyson took ruinous turns.

If you want to enhance your performance, submit yourself to others who care about your success. You should have mentors about whom you can say; "I like myself better because of the person you have helped me become." And when they hold you to a standard, thank them. You might consider performing unpleasant tasks or giving them money when they find you avoiding your commitment. Yes, it could be expensive, but how much will it cost if you don't follow through with your commitments? Plus, if you reward others when they catch you shirking a task, you'll be amazed at how concerned they become with your success.

There are consequences for not doing what we should. When I punish my children, I'm doing them a favor by teaching them that disobedience has costs. That's why they've never heard me say, "This is going to hurt me more than it hurts you." There is a term for children who haven't experienced consequences -- spoiled brats. There's a term for adults who avoid consequences and accountability -- frustrated wannabe's. **Livers of life embrace accountability** and agree that --

Hungry Buzzards Know Best.

Some live by the old saying, "Good things happen to those who wait." Though this statement has merit, when pursuing goals it's better to follow the example of the hungry buzzard that said, "I'm tired of waiting for an animal to die -- I'm gonna kill something!" **Patience is a virtue but not when it's an excuse for inaction**. Within reason we should feel a sense of urgency, a desire to press forward to completion. If you have to swallow a goldfish, it's best not to look at it too long.

An old bachelor friend of mine said he was waiting for God to find his mate because he was tired of "fishing" for a wife. I said, "That's fine but if you stop fishing... your bait will go stale!" Good things come by consistent action. Remember the disciples were not told to wait for people to come to them; they were instructed to go into the world and be "fishers of men." And remember, if you catch them, He'll clean them.

Hitler believed (and proved) if you tell the masses a lie loud enough and long enough eventually they accept it. Tragically, it's also true when we lie to ourselves. Perhaps the biggest lie we construct is that we'll have more time tomorrow. "I'll start exercising on Monday." "I'll work on my taxes later" "I'll look for a job next week." "I'll get serious about my commitment to God soon." "Honey, give me a break; I'll take out the garbage in a minute."

Anyone over thirty years old has experienced how quickly life passes. As you review your life, how much did procrastination cost you? As stated earlier, you can't change the past but it helps to remember the cost when flirting with postponement. Procrastinators are always playing catch up; like a one legged tuba player in a marching band. To avoid this syndrome, form the habit of training your mind to say "DO IT!" Shouting the words when you catch yourself avoiding action conditions your mind to act. Unless we are vigilant, our lazy nature seduces us like a moth to a flame. Whether the goals are large or small, when you start to procrastinate remember: **"Today is the tomorrow that yesterday you committed to change."**

Antiquity's Success Secret

Archeologist Indiana Bones was obsessed with acquiring an ancient scroll containing the pharaoh's secret of success. Its discovery had eluded mankind for 3000 years. To no avail, searchers studied the great manuscripts of scholars and philosophers from antiquity. Their quests took them on perilous journeys, into dark jungles, over stormy seas, and across scorching deserts. Many sacrificed all they owned in search of this secret of the ages.

After years of fruitless excavations in the Egyptian Desert, Indiana Bones was distraught. Taking a break from digging, he leaned on his shovel, a habit he learned as a former highway construction worker. The sand beneath his shovel suddenly collapsed, pulling him into a swirling vortex. Tumbling head over heels, he landed in an underground chamber. Lighting a torch, he peered through darkness and shivered at the sight before him.

them. Recognize that their motives are probably not intentionally harmful and evaluate their advice from that perspective.

Certainly some people want to stall your progress. They're reminiscent of the time I got stuck driving behind a long line of cars. The lead driver was in a smoke-belching old rusty truck. He apparently enjoyed creating the procession because he made passing difficult by speeding up on the straightaways. Finally, I maneuvered behind him and was irate to see a bumper sticker on his truck's rear window that read, "I MAY BE SLOW BUT I'M AHEAD OF YOU."

He was typical of those who fear others' advancement. Sometimes subtlety (or openly) such people will attempt to sabotage your designs. An Arab proverb teaches the appropriate response, "The dogs bark but the caravan moves on." Give the barkers in your life your keys and tell them to go to your house and take whatever they want. It's better that they steal your possessions instead of stealing your dreams. Let critics spur you on; see their comments as a hurdle that's fun to jump. Perhaps that's why Thomas Edison quipped, **"If you want to succeed, get some enemies."**

How Hard Is It To Achieve

Former Olympic decathlon winner Bob Richards said that he won the gold medal even though there were athletes who could run faster, throw farther, jump higher, and were stronger. The reason he beat these superior athletes was simple -- they never tried out. If you don't show up for dinner, you don't eat. You don't have to be leaps and bounds ahead of the competition to win. Victory often belongs to the man or woman who grits their teeth and hangs on a few minutes longer. Horse races are won by inches. Valedictorians are determined by a fraction of a grade point. Elections are won by a few votes. Jobs and promotions are often not awarded to the most intelligent person, but to the person who does the simple little extra things.

Booker T. Washington validated the "simple thing theory" by saying, "Success results from doing common things in an uncommon way." The solutions to most of the challenges we face are seldom complicated. When you don't know what else to try, simplify. For instance; I asked my dentist, "Doc, my teeth are turning yellow, what should I do?" He answered, "Wear a brown tie."

Winning Is Everything... Wrong

Winning doesn't always mean the victor is the sole benefactor. In business negotiations, the term "win-win" demonstrates there is frequently plenty of room on top, like a plateau. Many noteworthy companies never claim the majority of market share. Often great sports stars don't play on a championship teams. Accomplished singers rarely record number-one songs.

No one is capable of always being number one; eventually age, superior competition or misfortune catches up with the best of us. In referring to his slippery position as British Prime Minister, Benjamin Disraeli said, "I have climbed to the top of the greasy pole." Striving to be the best is admirable, but it's generally a temporary post. Noteworthy accomplishments are often achieved by average folks who aren't the best in their field, nor do they desire to be. Their satisfaction comes from giving their best.

There are things you can't achieve, but you can derive satisfaction from doing your best. Most golfers know they will never be pros or be able to shoot par. To keep the game interesting and to motivate themselves to improve, they establish an average score and strive to beat it. Since competition enhances our performance, we should never stop challenging ourselves. Even when we are no longer capable of breaking our own records, it's invigorating to see how close we can come. When Babe Ruth's career was nearing its end and his hitting ability was but a shadow of his past performances, he thrilled a crowd (and himself) by hitting four home runs in a single game.

A Famous Misquote

Some folks incorrectly attribute Coach Vince Lombardi as saying, "Winning isn't everything. It's the only thing." This is *not* what he said. Winning is not the only thing that counts. You gain any time you give 100% in pursuit of a goal, regardless of the outcome. You can learn as much from placing last as from taking the blue ribbon.

Sometimes victories make us overconfident, resulting in less preparation for our future competitions. What Vince Lombardi said is, "The **WILL** to win isn't everything; it's the only thing." There is all the difference in the world between these two statements. Lombardi didn't win all of his games. No one can. That's why he acknowledged that the **will** to win is the most important thing to possess. This **"will"** gives us the discipline to continue preparing whether we win or lose.

I know a guy who is an incredibly competitive racquetball player. He hollers, curses, throws his racket and often screams, "I would rather die than lose!" Though he frequently loses... he's still alive. He has the desire to win, but he loses because he doesn't have the desire to PRACTICE!

Of course, practice alone does not guarantee improvement. Renowned archer Fred Bear said that instead of shooting a group of arrows when practicing, it is more effective to shoot one arrow at a time. Then as you walk to the target to retrieve the arrow, think about what you did that was right and wrong. Shooting one arrow after another without a break often results in practicing bad habits, especially if you get tired and it affects your form. Practice does not make perfect. Perfect practice makes perfect.

The Plan is Everything

"In war", said Dwight Eisenhower, "the plan is everything, but nothing goes according to plan." Having specific plans makes it obvious when things go wrong, giving us time to make corrections. Achievers devise plans because they expect difficulties, not from a fearful, pessimistic perspective, but from a realistic understanding that adversity is all part of the process. Only a foolish boxer steps into the ring thinking he won't be hit. People who don't expect adversity are the first ones to throw in the towel, blame others, or make excuses. Livers of life search adversity knowledge. Washington won the Revolutionary War through seven years of brilliantly retreating. The lessons learned from licking their wounds on the run enabled the army in the eighth year to have a victorious outcome.

On D-Day many American soldiers jumped off their landing craft into water that was over their heads. The equipment they carried impaired their ability to swim. After struggling to stay afloat, some were so exhausted they couldn't tread water and they drowned. One soldier survived by allowing himself to sink to the bottom; then he squatted and pushed himself up and forward. Upon surfacing, he filled his lungs with air and sank to the bottom again. He repeated the process until he reached shallow water. **Sometimes we have to sink to the bottom before we can rise to the top.**

When Beethoven went deaf, his world of silence enabled him to focus even more on music. He composed great symphonies when he could hear them only in his imagination. 1960 Olympic triple gold medal sprinter, Wilma Rudolph, suffered the crippling effects of polio as a child. Surely this was largely responsible for creating her passionate desire to run. George Washington only had the equivalent of a third grade education. To compensate for his lack of schooling, he read over 900 books in a time when books were hard to acquire. For those with the heart to achieve, trying times are not a reason to quit; they are a reason to try.

General George Patton remarked, "You do not judge someone's success by how high they climb, you judge their success by how high they bounce when they fall." While addressing the House of Commons during WWII, Churchill warned, "I have never promised anything or offered anything but blood, tears, toil, and sweat, to which I will now add our fair share of mistakes, shortcomings and disappointments, and also that it may go on for a very long time, at the end of which I firmly believe -- though it is not a promise or a guarantee, only a profession of faith -- that there will be complete, absolute, and final victory." It would be difficult to find a better example of acknowledging adversity but maintaining the will to win.

We all grew up with the old adage, "If at first you don't succeed try, try again." That's not good enough. If at first you don't succeed, analyze why you didn't succeed. Turn the failure over and over in your mind. Pick it apart and poke it with a stick before you try again. Not only is it imperative to learn from our mistakes, it's also important to learn from others' mistakes. Comedian Stephen Wright suggested, "Being first is not always best; after all, it's the second rat that gets the cheese!"

Don't Jump and Stay On The Farm

In an interview with Diane Sawyer concerning his movie, *The Passion*, actor Mel Gibson said that he had been handed the pinnacle of success, money, and fame beyond what most could conceive. Gibson said that the eventual result was that he contemplated suicide by jumping out of a window. He says that faith restored his life since the world had nothing else to offer.

If success is determined by whatever one believes, then Osoma Bin Laden and Saddam Hussein are successes since they see no wrong in their actions. It's not beliefs, but truth that determines success, and God ultimately determines truth. Churchill said, "Men stumble over truth from time to time, but most pick themselves up and hurry off as if nothing happened." During the Lincoln-Douglass debates, Lincoln asked the audience, "How many legs would a horse have if you called his tail a leg?" "Five," shouted some onlookers. "Four," replied Lincoln. "Calling a tail a leg doesn't make it true." All of us have the prejudice of our desires, causing us to deny truth. And sometimes our finite minds simply can't discern His will.

While plowing, a farmer looked up into the sky and saw the clouds form two perfect letters, P.C. Instantly he new God was telling him to Preach Christ. He went to seminary, acquired a degree, and was hired by a small church. Five years and 250 sermons later, his congregation was even smaller than when he began. He resigned in frustration and went back to his farm. Preparing to plow, he again saw letters in the sky. This time the clouds specifically spelled, "Plant Corn"!

We frequently twist God's answers to fit our designs, or we ask the wrong questions when the answer is before us. When you feel confused, practice attributes you know are right such as discipline, courage, honesty, forgiveness, humility, and generosity. Frankly, **if we aren't doing the things we know are right, why should we expect additional divine guidance?**

How To Find God's Will In One Word

Imagine someone told you they believed in physical fitness. You asked about their exercise regimen and they said, "Well, I don't work out very often but I'm really into fitness." So you ask, "Do you read a lot about health issues?" "No," they respond, "I don't, but I really value fitness." "Oh, so you must eat properly?" you inquire. "No," they say, "I don't know much about nutrition and I frequently eat junk food." You ask, "So, you must belong to a health club and regularly discuss fitness issues with other advocates?" They snipe with pride, "I once attended a health club, but the members were all a bunch of hypocrites!"

Obviously such a person isn't really committed to physical fitness. Similarly, some claim to want to find God's purpose for their life, but there's no real commitment. Frankly that description fits me in my young adulthood. Since I rarely exercised my faith, studied, or prayed, I felt uncomfortable sharing my faith since there was so little to share. **My religion was so private; I didn't even inflict it on myself.** Though the answer was obvious, I wondered why I wasn't in tune with God's purpose. I wish God had gotten my attention with a cosmic size, "Duh!"

If you desire to develop spiritual discernment for the goals and decisions you make, if you want to derive more from your faith, put more into it. There's a shortcut to finding God's will, it results from a word that many avoid and some even scorn. The word is, **obedience.** "Seek first the kingdom of God, and His righteousness and all these things will come unto you."

Faith Enhances The Intellect

When he was running for president, Lincoln told a friend, "I know there is a God, and that He hates injustice and slavery. I see the storm coming, and I know that His hand is in it. If He has a place and work for me, I believe I am ready. I am nothing, but truth is everything." Despite the gravity of the circumstances Lincoln faced, God did not send him marching orders, yet Lincoln was confident his path was righteous. He had not always been so sure of God's designs. As a young man he was a skeptic, but through their obsessively focused nature excludes things like relaxed and meaningful conversation. They rank people on a scale of importance, which is based upon a person's ability to feed their egos, provide some service, or help them maintain their prestige. **If God were concerned with prestige, Jesus would have been born at the Ritz.**

Don't pursue a goal with such tunnel vision that you sacrifice your health, your sanity, and your relationships. It's foolish to have a room full of trophies and no one with whom to share your victories. How do you benefit if you are totally obsessed with a goal and after its attainment, you are left with emptiness? Jesus asked what good is it to gain the whole world and lose your soul. Ascribe to goals that help you maintain balance, not sacrifice it. If the world's success train is taking you to ruin, commandeer it, slam on the brakes, back up, and retrieve the important things you left behind. **God is not as concerned with our accomplishments as He is with our character.**

A Passion For Achievement

Don't mistake my advocacy of life balance as a passionless attitude about improving our performance or desiring victory. We should never lose our zeal for improvement to make the most of our talents. Olympic runner Eric Liddle said in the movie *Chariots of Fire* "God made me for a purpose, but he also made me fast, and when I run I feel God's pleasure." Victory is important, sometimes essential. The world's democracies would not exist today if the heroes who fought Hitler had said, "It's not whether you win or lose the war that counts, it's how you play the game." If there are no wins in business the result is bankruptcy and unemployment. Without righteous wins in court, the innocent are convicted and the guilty go unpunished. From beauty pageants to bull riding, the quest for victory brings out our best efforts.

Years ago I debated a group of students about the advantages of competitive free market over socialism. One student said that socialism was more humane because it assures that no one fails or falls behind. I said if you want to keep your classmates from failing, then add all of your test scores together, and the average grade is what everyone receives. "No!" they replied, except some football players who shouted, "That sounds great!"

Similarly, I took friendly issue with my son's soccer league because they thought the young children might be adversely affected by losing, so they didn't keep score. The policy's foolishness was exposed when the six-year-olds kept score on their own. The desire to win is hard-wired into our souls, and to deny our desire for victory is to assure mediocrity.

It's healthy to desire victory, but to base our esteem on its attainment is a recipe for a yo-yo self-worth. When we make a sale, get a promotion, or receive an "atta girl," we're on a high. When we fail to do so, the blues stick to us like flypaper. That's why our esteem should be built upon things we can influence, such as fulfilling our commitments, serving others, maintaining our integrity, and pursuing knowledge and faith. By allowing things within our control to influence our esteem, we net a more consistent confidence than basing our esteem on victories. **God doesn't require us to win -- only to strive.**

Monday Morning Blues

Some people don't understand why their enthusiasm about a goal can so quickly diminish. One reason is their motivation was too dependent upon emotion. **Contrary to what some people think, feelings are only part of motivation -- sometimes a very small part.**

Observe anyone who exercises daily. Often they don't feel like exercising, but their commitment is not dependent upon feelings. Feelings are not dependable instigators of action. The motivation of committed athletes is primarily dependent on one word: **discipline**. They force themselves to do the thing they committed to do regardless of their emotional state, and soon their enthusiasm returns. Character has been defined as the ability to follow through with a commitment, after the mood in which the commitment was made passes. When an emotionally down time overtakes you, recognize it for what it is -- your humanity. Everybody experiences it.

Lewis and Clark never found the Northwest Passage. Lincoln never saw the complete surrender of the South. Franklin Roosevelt died before seeing the defeat of the Nazis. Van Gogh only sold one of his paintings. After forty years of searching Moses wasn't allowed to live in the Promise Land. John Kennedy never witnessed his goal of an American on the moon. Still, unfinished dreams aren't necessarily tragic. Michelangelo prayed, "Lord grant that I may always desire more than I can accomplish." I certainly hope to live long enough to see my children raise their families, but if my life ends tomorrow, what an honor and joy it's been to guide their paths thus far. Life doesn't always allow us to see the conclusions we seek, but throughout your life, **you have the privilege of the quest.**

Value Your Gifts

You are God's greatest creation. You were born at a specific time for significant purposes. You're not a bowling pin waiting to be bashed, a hapless victim of fate, or a cog in a wheel. To be unaware of your value is more wasteful than burning a virgin forest. You are more unique than the greatest work of art. The Mona Lisa smiles, but unlike you, she can't laugh. When Michelangelo completed his sculpture of Moses, he gazed upon the perfection of his masterpiece and striking it with a hammer he screamed, "Speak!" The magnificent statue could only answer with silence.

You're more complex than the Internet; it can't think or create. You're more valuable than a galaxy; planets don't feel compassion, stars can't see, and comets don't sing. The Grand Canyon has no dream, the Sphinx doesn't love, and the Nile is unable to reverse its direction. You can change your course, alter your character, and expand your life. The next time you look at a masterpiece, the glories of nature, or the infinity of the universe, stand tall and shout, **"You think you're something, take a look at me!!**

Your life is a splendid mirror. Its reflection shines upon others and will impact generations yet to be born. For that reason, be an advocate for true and good things. Filter your life through the screen of an honorable character. Hone your convictions; don't just think about them, live them, teach them, and carry them wherever you go.

Never forget the story of the woman who told her priest that each night God paid her a visit and they talked. Skeptically the priest said, "If that is true, then ask Him what was the last sin for which I asked forgiveness." They met the next day and the priest inquired, "Did you ask God what sin I confessed?" She said, "Yes I did." Smugly he replied, "And what was that sin?" The woman answered, "God said He did not remember." Indeed, Hebrews 8:12 says that when we ask God's forgiveness He will grant it and His memory of that sin will be no more.

When you fail to practice your ideals, when you do, say, or think what you shouldn't -- learn from the error and seek redemption. Each morning God's "tender mercies" are renewed. Arise and know that you are capable of amazing change and astonishing things. Your past failures, present storms, and future battles are not as formidable as the spirit within you. **Your greatest weakness can become your greatest strength.**